MIRACLES AND GHOSTS

A CHRISTMAS COLLECTION

D. L. FINN

Library of Congress Control Number: 2024918767

eBook ISBN: 979-8-9861587-9-2

Paperback ISBN: 979-8-9914071-0-6

ALSO BY D. L. FINN

Evildwel/Angel Series

This Second Chance (Book 1)

The Button: This Only Chance (Book 2)

This Last Chance (Book 3)

Companion Evildwel/Angel Stories

A Long Walk Home: A Christmas Novelette

Red Eyes in the Darkness: A Short Story

I Wouldn't Be Surprised: A Short Story

Paranormal Historical Fiction

Sounds in the Silence

Paranormal Thriller

A Voice in the Silence

Short Story Collection

In the Tree's Shadow

Miracles and Ghosts: A Christmas Collection

Other Short Stories

Bigfoot: A Short Story

Novelette

The Destination: Harbor Pointe Series Book 3

Poetry

Just Her Poetry Seasons of a Soul

Deep in the Forest Where Poetry Blooms: Just Her Poetry Book Two

Children's Books (middle grade)

Elizabeth's War (historical fiction)

An Unusual Island (fantasy)

Things on a Tree (holiday / fantasy)

Dolphin's Cave (fantasy)

Tree Fairies and Their Short Stories (fantasy)

ACKNOWLEDGMENTS

A huge thank you and hug goes out to my patient beta readers Sandra and Yvette. Your feedback was a gift! Thank you to Denise at *Artful Editor* for making my words readable.

All my love goes to my husband, family, friends, and writing community, whose patient support and encouragement kept me going.

Finally, to my readers, thank you for joining me on this magical holiday excursion!

CHAPTER 1
A PERFECT GHOSTLY CHRISTMAS NOVELETTE

JULIE SANDALS PULLED in to the gravel driveway of the old ranch house where she used to live with her grandparents. It stood defiantly against the harsh winter elements of the Sierra Nevada foothills. Years had dulled the cheerful yellow paint. Someone had boarded up a broken window like slapping on a Band-Aid, and rusty moss had taken up residence on the roof. The landscape was slowly reclaiming what once was a loving family home.

She sighed, threw the old Chevy Nova into park, turned the key, and heard it shudder off.

"What am I supposed to do, Grams? I wish you could send me a sign or perhaps a—"

Julie leaned forward and wiped the dirty windshield with her lime-green fleece sleeve. A pristine rainbow had appeared, ending in the once-thriving apple orchard behind the house. "Wow! A perfect rainbow! I remember you loved them, Grams, and said seeing them meant something good was coming. Are you trying to tell me there's a pot of gold waiting for me at the end?"

A hollow laugh escaped Julie's lips, betraying her true feelings. Grams was dead and wasn't sending her rainbows or anything else. Still, odd things always happened around her, like items vanishing and reappearing where she had just searched. It meant nothing and hadn't changed her situation since the day her world shifted.

The memory of her last Christmas at this house kept Julie going through the dark years of foster care and the loneliness of college. Now she was a responsible, logical adult with a shiny new teaching degree and an old house she inherited last month on her twenty-fifth birthday. Only this building, the land, and $152 after the lawyers' fees remained from those who had loved her. Her heart wanted to hang on to it, but how could she?

She longed to return to her innocent eight-year-old self, still believing that Santa existed and everything would be all right. But nothing was all right, and she had no power to alter it.

"If only that hadn't happened. If only . . . "

CHAPTER 2
DECEMBER 1969

JULIE SNUGGLED into her cozy red flannel sheets, unable to sleep. Although the day had raced by filled with anticipation, the minutes spent trying to sleep dragged on as she awaited Christmas morning. Her mind wandered back to her perfect busy day.

"How does this look, Grams?" She pointed to a gingerbread cookie shaped like a snowman.

Her grandmother's loving smile showed behind a mask of concentration as she decorated cookies that were too pretty to eat. "Perfect! Decorate it later after it cools."

"He needs a face and hat, and I can use thin licorice as his arms." Julie grinned, showing off her missing front tooth.

"Santa will be thankful for that gesture. You better get ready for church now. We don't want to be late." Grams winked and concentrated on the carefully applied white lace design on her gingerbread cookies.

Julie raced up the wooden stairs. Soon she was sitting in church wearing her sparkly red holiday dress with black shoes that were on the snug side after her last growth spurt. She couldn't focus on the sermon with gifts waiting for her under the Christmas tree. Only her favorite part at the end—when they sang the special holiday songs—

pulled her back to reality. Her voice was loud and clear and drew a couple of smiling glances.

Gramps, Grams, and Julie didn't linger to visit.

"You should join the choir someday, Julie. You can sure sing," Gramps said as he pulled into their gravel driveway.

"She sure can." Grams nodded.

"I want to." If she ever gathered the courage to sing in front of a crowd.

"Come help me with dinner, Julie. Wear one of my aprons and keep that pretty red lace clean," Grams said.

"Tortellini soup?"

"You bet, with freshly grated mozzarella and my special sourdough bread smothered in butter from the Rodgers' farm." Grams tied on her worn flowered apron.

"And dessert?" Intense hunger washed over Julie, causing her mouth to water with anticipation.

"A Texas sheet cake that needs your touch with the green and red sprinkles. And our cookies need decorating, especially Santa's cookies. I didn't have time after I got the cookies ready to share with neighbors. Now let's get started while Gramps hangs the stockings for Santa."

After dinner Julie opened one gift. It was a green snowflake night-gown that twisted around her, making her feel like a swaddled baby. The day had been amazing, and she couldn't let it go. She hopped out of bed and peeked out the blue-and-white striped drapes, hoping to spot Santa's sleigh. As if on cue, it began to snow.

"You must be coming, Santa. I hope you like our cookies. I did the snowman."

Footsteps echoed down the long wooden hall toward her room. Julie closed the drapes tightly, leaving behind the biting chill. She dove under the covers and closed her eyes, pretending to be asleep.

After the soothing echo of her grandparents' footsteps subsided, her door opened quietly.

"She's finally fallen asleep," Grams said.

"Dreaming of sugarplum fairies, I bet," Gramps whispered.

Julie kept her eyes squeezed closed as gentle kisses covered her exposed cheek.

"Merry Christmas, little one." The warm presence was gone, and her door closed with a loud click and the special holiday shadows filled her room.

Finally she dozed off into her last peaceful slumber.

Dawn peeked through her curtains, nudging Julie awake. She jumped up and threw them open. The landscape was covered in white as if someone had sprayed it with whipped cream. "Hooray!"

Her stomach growled as she tugged on her pink slippers and robe. She raced down the cold, wooden stairs to the glowing, flocked tree covered in tinsel. The stockings were lumpy and weighed down. Crumbs left on the plate and an empty glass proved Santa had visited. Tucked away behind the tree was a sparkly pink bicycle with a green bow draped over it.

Shouting with joy, Julie announced, "Guess what? Santa has come!" She wanted to ride the bike but knew she'd have to wait for her grandparents to be there.

"You don't say! Merry Christmas!" Grams peeked in from the kitchen, holding morning coffee in her favorite sky-blue mug.

Julie raced into her arms. "Merry Christmas!"

"Careful now, coffee's hot. Gramps will be in soon. He's checking on the animals. I have your breakfast ready for you, then we'll see what Santa brought."

"A bike!" Julie plopped in front of a plate of scrambled eggs and pancakes. She didn't even taste the food she gobbled down.

"Don't choke, sweetheart." Grams shook her head, and her braided salt-and-pepper hair waved over her shoulder, free from its usual bun in a sign of holiday rebellion. "Your gifts aren't going anywhere."

"I know. I'm so excited! I can ride my bike to school with Tessa and Tommy. We'd be safe with Tessa's big brother."

Grams crossed her arms tightly across her chest. "We'll see. Maybe on some days, but Gramps loves to drive you."

"He does, but it would save him the gas." Julie offered the wide-eyed look that usually worked.

"We'll talk about that later. First, you need to wash your breakfast down with some orange juice." Grams smoothed her red plaid holiday apron and glanced out the window. Julie swiftly complied.

That perfect Christmas morning raced by with the same blurry speed as the roller coaster at the fair last summer. The colorful wrapping paper and ribbon lay in piles.

Gramps glanced at Grams. "Santa must have known how good you were this year. Never seen a little girl get this much for Christmas."

"Yes, a bike by the tree and fashion dolls in your sock. Lucky girl," Grams said.

"I named her Tandy and her little sister Lucy. They were just what I wanted. They have blue dresses like mine. How did Santa know?"

"Santa knows those kinds of things," Grams said.

"He sure does," Gramps patted Grams's hand.

Julie held up the sky-blue dress with a white collar that her grandparents had given her. "The dress is the best, and the shoes look like the ones in the catalog. You remembered! Can I wear them to Tessa's house for dinner?"

Grams wore a smile, radiating joy. "I'm glad to hear you like it. Of course you can wear your new outfit. I can't wait to see it on you. That blue matches your eyes."

Julie paged through her new book, *A Wrinkle in Time*. Tessa had told her about it, and she couldn't wait to read it.

She hardly noticed what her grandparents received other than what she crafted for them at school: new red plaid oven mitts for Grams and a brown ceramic ashtray for when Gramps smoked his stinky cigars.

Excitement grew as dinner at Tessa's family's house approached. Julie was eager to show off her new dress.

They piled into Gramps's red pickup because all the wheels operated together instead of just two, making it easier to maneuver in the snow.

"Sure is strange not cooking Christmas dinner," Grams said as she climbed into the truck with Gramps's help. She wore her best dress, the one with tiny blue flowers that Gramps loved.

"Honey, I believe it's high time for you to take a well-deserved break. It'll be nice to enjoy the Rodgers' hospitality."

"True, but I brought your favorite pumpkin pie."

Gramps tugged at his dress shirt collar and started the truck. "You spoil me."

Grams couldn't hide her pleased expression as she snapped the seat belt across her lap. "Just a pie. Now, be careful, Jack, it's icy."

He gripped the steering wheel with both hands and winked at Grams. "I always am, Margie. Always am—right, Julie?" His white mustache couldn't hide his grin.

"Always, Gramps. Thank you for letting me bring the bike. Tessa rides hers in the barn when it snows." She sat Tandy and Lucy next to her.

Gramps nodded but never took his dark blue eyes off the road. "I'm going to ask Stan if it's okay before I take it out. The tarp will keep the bike safe either way."

Right before they made the turn into her best friend's driveway, there was a loud cracking and popping sound.

"Jack!" Grams screamed.

The brakes squealed as Julie's seat belt tightened, making it hard to catch her breath. The beautiful oak tree, adorned with colorful bulbs, was falling toward them. Then it hit. The roof above her grandparents buckled under its weight.

"Grams! Gramps!" Julie gasped right before her head slammed against the back window and everything disappeared.

She awakened in an unfamiliar bed with what looked like a clear straw taped to her right arm. The sterile white drapes couldn't keep out the reality of those last moments before—

But she was alive, which meant her grandparents had to be too. She tried to sit but found wires taped to her chest, and her left arm was in a white cast. She gingerly tried to move her legs. Her right one, like her arm, moved easily, but her left was heavy like her casted arm.

"Help!" she called out.

No one came.

Julie took a deep breath. "I need help!"

The beige door flung open, and an older lady in a white skirt and blouse entered carrying a chart. She murmured, "My name is Miss Ruby. I'm here to help you, honey. Are you in any pain?"

"Pain? No. Is my arm broken?"

After studying the chart, Miss Ruby spoke. "Your left arm and leg are fractured, but they will heal fast. There's some chest bruising from the seat belt, and you have a bump on your head that needs to be monitored. You should recover nicely. Would you like some water?"

Dry-mouthed, Julie nodded. After the liquid soothed her throat, talking became easier. "Thank you. I'd like to see my grandparents now."

Miss Ruby pursed her lips together. "I just came on duty. After I take your vitals, I'll find out where they are."

After a silent examination, Julie took the offered pain pill.

"Should you require anything, press the button." Without a backward glance, Ruby nodded and swiftly exited the room.

Julie emerged from a haze when the round-the-clock pills ceased and she could open her eyes fully. Despite the discomfort, she pressed the button.

An older woman with bright red hair entered the room. "Hello, my name is Mrs. Gober. Are you in any pain?"

Julie shook her head.

Mrs. Gober sank into the chair next to Julie, grabbed a fresh tissue from the box on the little table, and clasped it in her manicured hand. "I'm glad to hear that. I can call the nurse for you at any time if you feel discomfort. I'm here to answer questions you might have."

"Did my grandparents get hurt in the crash too? Is that why they aren't here?"

The plump woman smoothed her stylish beehive hairstyle. She smelled like the mix of perfumes she and Grams used to test at Briver's department store. "Yes, sweetheart. Do you remember what happened?"

"We were going to the Rodgers' for dinner. A tree began to fall, and Gramps swerved, but it still landed on the truck. I don't remember anything after that. When can I see Grams and Gramps?"

Mrs. Gober pursed her lips. "That bump knocked you out." She wrote something on the paper. Her lipstick bore a striking resemblance to blood and had left streaks on her teeth. "That's *all* you remember?"

"Yes."

"Do you have any other family we should contact? Your neighbors didn't know of any."

Julie's head throbbed. "Only my grandparents. Are they going to be okay? Can I go see them?"

Mrs. Gober's blue eyes were cold and hard, like those of the man who had wanted to buy their house. She had never seen Gramps so adamant about someone leaving their home. Julie's stomach churned and her chest tightened like it had that day when she saw her beloved Gramps get mad. Mrs. Gober placed an icy hand on Julie's shoulder and delivered the news that changed her life forever.

"Sorry. No. They went to heaven. I'll ensure you find a good home after you're released." Mrs. Gober handed Julie a tissue that couldn't absorb the pain that poured down her face. She was utterly alone.

CHAPTER 3
DECEMBER 1986

THOSE MEMORIES WERE JUST as painful now. Julie wiped away the free-flowing tears that released her past and sighed.

"Home," she murmured and opened the car door. What did it mean after all this time?

She trudged through the weed-covered front yard that used to be Grams's beautiful garden. The familiar red front door still had the rusty Christmas bell wreath hanging on the nail Gramps had hammered into Grams's recently painted door, which was now peeling. To say Grams wasn't happy about it was a vast understatement. Gramps didn't know she'd bought a fancy new hook to put over the top of the door. Julie had helped add the red and green ribbons that year. Now it had a spiderweb, making it more like a decoration for Halloween. Wood for the stove, with a note on top, was stacked neatly to the left of the door.

Dearest Julie,

We were thrilled to hear that you were coming home today. Welcome! We've kept an eye on the house for you and taken care of turning on the power and phones for your return. Thought you could use some wood since the heater wasn't working when we closed the house. You might need a new one. The woodstove will keep you warm, and if you need any more wood, we have plenty to share. Still have the key your grandma left, so we cleaned the fridge and left some salt, pepper, eggs, coffee, bananas, a casserole, bread, butter, bologna, mustard, canned food, dishwashing liquid, toilet paper, and cleaning supplies to help settle you. If you need anything, we are here for you. Our phone number is on the fridge. We've missed you, and we're eager to see you soon.

Love,
Pearl Rodger

Julie frowned and tucked the note into her pocket. "Missed me? You didn't bother to visit me at the hospital, offer to take me in, or even contact me all these years. At least it explains why the power company said I had already called in for service. A little guilt, Mrs. Rodger?" She shook her head and unlocked the door.

It creaked open, and Julie switched on the entry light, which bathed the house in a musty, yellowish glow. Nothing had changed except for the dusty sheets laid over the furniture, which she snatched off and tossed to the side. The house was cozy, with a yellow kitchen, woodstove, family room, red velvet couches, a round wooden accent table by Gramps's seat, and red gingham curtains by Grams's. She opened the window that wasn't broken to air the place out and established a crackling fire to burn off the years of disuse. Wooden stairs led to the three bedrooms and a second bath, an area she wasn't ready to explore yet.

With all the cleaning products and the mop left behind, Julie spent the day scrubbing and cleaning. Her last chore was to vacuum. Over by the front window were a couple of brown pine needles from their Christmas tree from so many years ago. She tossed them in the trash and sighed. Exhausted, she plopped onto the couch and fell asleep.

She awoke to a world cloaked in darkness. Her stomach growled, and the stove needed more wood.

She tried turning on the stovetop. "Darn, I forgot about the propane. That explains why the water never heated. I'll call tomorrow and get it delivered. Guess I'm cooking on the woodstove, like we used to do when the power went out—before we got a fancy gas stove that needed propane."

The lasagna was warm in no time. It was as good as she remembered from eating over at Tessa's house. It had been her home away from home until— She shoved the final cheesy bite into her mouth and cleaned her dirty dishes in cold water.

"Not much else to do but go to bed." Julie sighed and lay on the couch. Tomorrow she'd go upstairs. The grandfather clock struck nine, making her jump as it melodiously announced the hour. "Funny, I didn't wind it up. Maybe Mrs. Rodger did, and I didn't notice it ringing. Or I did it without thinking? Long day. Well, nine used to be my bedtime." She glanced at the old clock. The pendulum swayed serenely. "I'll turn the sound off like you used to do at night, Grams." She clicked the switch off and fell into an exhausted sleep.

Julie awakened to the clock chiming seven. "That's when you used to turn it back on, Grams. Has a mind of its own, I guess." She yawned, pulled the covers over her head, and was fast asleep again.

A knock pulled her from slumber. She tugged on a pink bathrobe and flung open the door.

"I'm Bob, here for your propane delivery, ma'am. All your connections have been checked, and everything is still in good working order. I need to come inside to light the water heater and stove. They told me the central heater was shut off because it was broken, but I'll double-check for you."

"I was going to call—oh, did Mrs. Rodger call?"

Bob frowned at the paper in his hands, which had more hair on them than his bald head. "I don't have a name, only an address. You wanted propane, didn't you?"

Julie opened the screen and waved him in. "Yes, I certainly do. Please come in."

"I should have asked first. We filled the wrong house a few years back. The situation was a mess, but they received free propane in the end. Point me in the right direction, and I'll get everything going for you."

Soon Julie had hot water, a functioning stove, and a broken heater.

"You're good to go. Sign here. Julie Sandals, right?"

"Yes. This was my grandparents' house." Julie signed on the dotted line.

"I remember Jack and Margie Winsome well from church. It's a shame about what happened. Good people. Welcome back home, and I hope you drop by the church sometime. Call when you need a refill, or we could put you on our regular route. Up to you. Here's our card so you can let Grace at the office know."

Immediately after Julie finished showering and getting dressed, there was a second knock at the door.

"Popular today," Julie murmured as the clock struck nine.

She ran a brush through her tangled hair and rushed to the door. She opened it to two men. The younger one had a brown mullet, a narrow black leather tie, a white shirt, a leather coat, and black slacks. The older man was dressed more formally in a dark suit.

"Miss Sandals? Miss Julie Sandals?" the older man asked.

Her body shivered as a chill ran down her spine. She would put on a warmer shirt after they left. "Yes, can I help you?"

"I'm Doug Gober, and this is my son, Doug Junior, from Gober Valley Realty. We heard you were coming home. Welcome back. Mr. and Mrs. Winsome were respected in our community."

Something tugged at the side of her memories. "Thank you. What can I do for you?"

He smiled and pushed back his greased salt-and-pepper hair while his son stood there like a bored child. She sweated like she was over-heating. Was she coming down with something?

"It's what we can do for *you*. The house holds little value, but the land may be valuable to someone. As luck would have it, there's a buyer interested in your property. It's truly amazing, don't you think? Cash deal, and we could close it for you by the first of the year." Doug handed her a card with their picture on it. The son appeared more engaged there.

A loud crash behind her made Julie turn her head to see what was happening. Her coffee cup lay shattered on the ground. "Oh, dear."

"You okay?" Doug Jr. said, his blue eyes narrowed.

Julie couldn't wait to get away from these two money-hungry sharks. "My cup was probably placed too close to the edge. I don't know what I'm doing, but I'll get back to you soon."

"I'd take this offer sooner rather than later. They're eager to close, and this could set you up nicely. Here's the offer for you to read. Let me know what you decide, but honestly, you won't get another offer like this one." Mr. Gober held out several papers that she accepted.

"I'll examine them later. Thanks for dropping by." Julie firmly shut the door before he could push anymore.

Doug Gober reminded her of a car salesperson. The offer was only good for today. If you walk out the door, it's gone. The speckled blue cup had been Grams's favorite. It now lay in pieces on the floor.

"Guess selling would be for the best." Julie reached for the broom.

The clock chimed five times, but it was nine thirty. "Clock must need an adjustment." She tossed the old cup in the trash and wiped away a tear. "I miss you, Grams."

The grandfather clock's pendulum abruptly stopped swinging. A sudden icy gust caught the papers from the realtor as a kitchen cabinet flew open. The gust was gone as fast as it came.

"Must be coming in from the window. Better have someone reseal it." She shut the cabinet and picked up the papers.

The offer was impressive, but what was the rush to buy an old house? However, it would pay off her debt and leave enough to put a down payment on a house back home. Home? Was that her home, or was it this town? The kitchen cabinet door flew open again, but with no icy gust this time. She felt around the window. There was no air seeping in, and the orchard leaves were still. No breeze.

"A ghost? No, that's silly." Julie shook her head and peered inside. Just dishes. "Wait, what's that?" She pulled out a yellowed piece of paper from the back, under all the dishes, and studied it carefully. "Oh."

She sank into a wooden kitchen chair. She was sitting on an actual gold mine. According to the paper from the county, her grandparents owned the mineral rights on their property. A report confirmed the two-ounce samples were indeed gold. The final document was a map with a notation of a large gold vein and a tunnel leading to it. A warning in red: *shore up old mine for safety*.

"This is crazy! Although I remember Gramps digging a new well for the orchard. He must have found it then. Wait, is this right?" The report's date caught her off guard. It was dated a week before they died. If the tree falling hadn't been an accident, she would have wondered about the timing.

She studied the papers in front of her. "I wonder if I missed anything." She pushed away from the table and inspected the cabinet one more time. The corner of another paper appeared under a blue plate in the back. "There *is* more."

Her curiosity was piqued as she removed the rest of the plates from the cabinet and held the last paper that had been hidden away all these years.

She frowned as she read it. "You've got to be kidding!" The person who wanted to buy her land now had made the same offer to her grandparents.

"I remember Gramps throwing Doug Gober out of the house that night. I wonder if the buyers are aware of the gold mine."

Another knock at the door. Julie quickly concealed the papers and replaced the dishes.

"Better not be those Realtors again," she mumbled.

She forcefully swung the door open, prepared to order them to leave, only to be faced with Mrs. Rodger, much older than she remembered.

"Julie! You look exactly like your mama. Welcome home." She gathered Julie into a powerful hug.

The first hug she'd had since her grandma died felt authentic, but if it truly was, why had Mrs. Rodger never made the effort to visit? With a swift motion, Julie pulled away. "Mrs. Rodger. Good to see you. Thank you for all you did for my return. Won't you come in?"

Mrs. Rodger couldn't hide the pain in her eyes. Julie felt guilty —almost.

"Julie, I am here and eager to help you with anything you need. And please call me Pearl. Did I see those Gobers leaving here?"

Julie shut the door as Pearl removed her fluffy blue coat and meticulously laid it over a chair. "Yes. They said someone wanted to buy the house."

"Did they say who?"

"The company is named Smith and Tucker Corporation. It's a generous offer."

Pearl sucked in her breath. "Are they still interested in buying? They offered your grandparents a hefty amount to sell, but they didn't want to sell. They planned to share good news before . . . "

"Before they died?"

Pearl's eyes watered. "Yes."

Julie couldn't hold inside what had been festering for years. "I was raised in foster homes. I had hoped—"

Pearl wiped the tears away and put a hand on Julie's shoulder. "I wanted to take you in, but because I was a widow with six children already, it wasn't allowed. They wouldn't let me see you, said it was for the best. You were wanted, trust me."

Julie gasped. "They wouldn't allow—wait, a widow?"

"You don't know?"

"Know what? How did you become a widow?"

Pearl pointed to the couch and sank into it. Julie sat next to her and waited. "After we heard the crash, Stan rushed out to see what it was. I told the kids to stay in the house and followed. By the time I got there, he had pulled you out of the truck and laid you safely away from the wreck. You had some broken bones, and I was grateful you weren't awake. I did what I could for you while Stan went back to your grandparents. There was a loud boom. I swear to this day it sounded like an explosion, and . . . "

Pearl paused and took a deep breath. Julie grasped her hand, and Pearl continued, "The rest of the tree fell. It crushed the three of them, and it would have killed you too, if not for Stan. He bravely saved your life that day but lost his." Pearl grabbed a white hanky from her pocket and blew her nose before continuing. "A car accident took your parents away from you, and a tree took your grandparents, but I had family left, and you didn't. I hope you know I didn't abandon you."

"I am so sorry for your loss. I didn't know, I swear. I thought no one wanted me."

Pearl rubbed her temples. "My concern was that you might perceive it that way. There were supposed to be papers with us named as your guardians, but no one found any record of them. If there were any, they were destroyed in a fire at their lawyer's office. I had no legal claim. I sent you gifts and letters, but they were all returned. I believed you had been adopted and had a new life. It was wrong of me to stop trying, but working and raising six kids alone kept me busy—although a seventh child wouldn't have added to my burden.

"My heart broke when I heard your last name hadn't changed. Still, part of me hoped your new parents let you keep your name. You're welcome at my house anytime. Tessa lives in New York with her husband, but she'll be home in a few days. She's eager to see you. Tommy helps me run the business now. The others stayed nearby and will all be present for Christmas. Of course, I want you to join us for Christmas. You will, won't you?"

Julie stared into the kind hazel eyes and careworn face that showed the burden she had carried since that day. Her heart melted as she gathered her neighbor in a hug. "I can't believe they kept you from me. Why?"

"I asked them that often. They never had an answer, other than it was the rules."

With a firm grip, Julie held on to Pearl, never wanting to release her. The winter that had held her heart for the last seventeen years was finally melting into spring.

Pearl pulled away and blew her nose on the Kleenex that Julie remembered she always kept in her pocket. She had lost so much too. They both had.

"Thank you. I feel better knowing," Julie said.

"I'm glad, sweetheart. You aren't alone anymore. Whatever you need, we're here for you. Got it?"

"Got it."

"Good. I took the day off, and I'm here to help you tidy up. Tommy found a great price on a heater this morning, from a site that doesn't want it. He assured me it would be perfect here. He'll be by after Christmas to install it, okay?" Pearl said.

"You are too kind to me, and I'll pay you back." Julie almost told her about the gold, but what if she was being nice because she knew about it? What if this was all an act? She couldn't think about that right now. Later.

"No hurry. Our company is doing good. I'm about ready to retire and enjoy life. What about you? Where do you work?"

"Nowhere. I graduated from college with a teaching degree. I specialize in middle school English and history. I'm going to job hunt after Christmas."

"Are you going to stay around here?" Pearl furrowed her brow.

"I hadn't planned on it, but being here feels like home. I'll give it some thought."

"That's because it is home. I know the principal and the school board very well. I heard a sixth-grade teacher, Mrs. Graham, is retiring at the end of the year. I bet they would let you substitute until then. Let me know if you want to check into it. Have you cleaned upstairs yet?" The little table at the top of the stairs was where keys and gloves used to end up was still covered.

"No, never made it there yesterday."

"I'll help you."

Julie sighed softly. "I can do it."

"Nonsense. It's why I'm here, to help."

"Thanks." She followed Pearl up the stairs.

Pearl took the mop into the green bathroom. Julie imagined the seahorses still hung on the wall over the towels with shells on them. So many memories were here. Her past weighed her feet down, and she couldn't move beyond the top of the stairs into the hall leading to her old bedroom.

"You can do this," she mumbled.

"What, dear?" Pearl peeked out the bathroom door. She appeared to notice every detail. Her piercing hazel eyes missed nothing. "You okay?"

"Yes. It's a lot, you know?"

"I do." Pearl's expression was full of concern. "I can clean if you aren't ready yet."

Julie wanted to take her offer, but it was time, wasn't it? "No, give me a moment. I'll be fine. Thanks, though."

Pearl placed a gentle hand on her shoulder. "If you want to talk, I'm always here for you."

Right then the grandfather clock started chiming, but it didn't stop at eleven. It went to twelve. "I think the clock needs to be fixed. Plus, it's louder than I remember."

"Tommy has a friend who works on clocks. I'll get his number from him." Pearl squeezed her shoulder and let go. She went back to her cleaning, which left Julie alone again.

Julie removed the sheet covering the table. She expected to see gloves sitting there, but it was bare. Sunbeams exited her room and landed on the worn wood of the hall floor in front of her like a light-house on a dark, frosty night, illuminating her path. She took a deep breath and moved toward the beams of light and her past.

Nothing had changed from the last night she had slept there, except the double bed had no linens, only a mattress cover. The brass head-board gleamed under the winter sun, the same scroll pattern that had fascinated her as a young girl. She believed it unlocked a world where fairies and magic thrived. The same faded blue-and-white drapes hung over the window that offered a view of the front yard and her old car. She'd lacked the Chevy that night, but everything else remained unchanged.

A clumsy painting of a sunflower hung above a scarred oak desk. Grams was so proud of it, insisted she'd never seen such talent in a third-grader. She asked Gramps to make a frame for it, which he planned to do after the holidays. Pushpins secured posters featuring kittens, fairies, unicorns, and wild horses. *A Wrinkle in Time* was on the nightstand next to the powder-blue lamp. A half-eaten candy cane lay where Julie had left it on Christmas Eve in 1969, and red tinsel was wrapped around the mirror above the five-drawer dresser. She peeked inside.

All the drawers were empty. Child Services came and got Julie's clothes but took nothing else. All her books, dolls, and toys were still in the blue box next to the desk. Tandy and Lucy had been taken out of the truck with her. They permitted her to bring only them into the foster home. At one point, a bigger girl took them from her. She learned it was better to have nothing but the clothes on her back in those homes. No one there cared about her belongings or her circumstances. She'd had to grow up fast, but now that little girl's life was right before her.

It was as if the room was a time capsule. She expected Grams to call her for lunch. She flopped onto the soft bed, but a cloud of dust puffed, and she sneezed loudly.

"Bless you!" Pearl shouted from the bathroom.

"Thank you." Not the voice the little girl desired to hear.

Adult Julie pushed those feelings down and removed the posters. She rolled them, using paper clips from the desk to secure them, and stacked them in the closet that contained sheets, a mattress pad, and the flowered quilt Grams made for her after her parents died on another icy road. She barely remembered her parents because she was only two years old when they died.

Again she was the sole survivor of a car accident. She was either unlucky or lucky, depending on how you looked at it. After she dusted, polished the wood, vacuumed the blue throw rugs and mattress, and cleaned the wood floor and the windows, the room was ready for her to use again. She shook out the amazingly fresh-smelling sheets and made the bed. She would sleep here tonight.

Pearl peeked in. "Looks good. I hope you don't mind that I washed your sheets and a few towels at home. They were dusty."

"I appreciate you doing that."

"You bet. Your washer and dryer still work—I checked, but it was easier for me to do it at home. Might want to run the washer before you use it. Your grandfather was going to move the washer and dryer out of the barn to the house, but your grandma wouldn't hear of it. He ran the electricity off the kitchen if you want to move them someday. I haven't touched your grandparents' room or yours, other than what those people took for you and what I washed. I thought you'd wanna go through them yourself."

"Yes, it's time I do this. I'll do my grandparents' room later, thanks." Julie's finger traced the windowsill, content with its new cleanliness.

"I cleaned the guest room too. If you decide to take up sewing, there's a nice sewing machine and material, thread, needles, scissors, and patterns inside the dresser," Pearl said. "It's way past lunch. How about I make us some sandwiches?"

"I'm not that hungry, but I'd be happy to make you one." Julie attempted to take the hostess role.

"Nonsense. I'll make us lunch. You can always eat it later."

The day flew by in pleasant company. They cleaned the oven and stairs, and then they headed to the barn. Musty old hay greeted them, left over from Lulu, the one cow they used to have, and an empty chicken coop. They never got the horse they'd always talked about. The washer and dryer were white with some rust on the outside, but the insides were clean. The box freezer, though, had seen better days, and it was time to retire it. Gramps's tools for the orchard hung, orderly, on the wall over a well-used tool chest. The tractor remained covered.

"Does the—" Julie paused when a sound came from the dark corner.

"What was that?" Pearl peered into the shadows. "I hope it isn't rats."

"Ew, I hope not." Julie grabbed a hammer, doubtful she'd use it unless attacked. The two women slowly approached the corner like brave warriors.

Julie didn't expect what she saw. "Oh . . . look."

"Well, I'll be. You have yourself a mouser and some babies."

Pearl bent over the small family. The small gray tiger-striped cat purred as three matching striped kittens nursed with vigor.

"How did you get in here? I'm surprised I didn't see you before." Pearl grabbed a small container and filled it with water from the sink by the washer and dryer. "I was just at the feed and supply before I dropped by. I have some cat food for our barn cats in my truck that I can share with you until you can get to the store. Unless you don't want them. I could take them with me."

"I've always wanted a kitten but never had the opportunity.

Grams was allergic. Made her sneeze like crazy. I want to keep at least the mom and find good homes for the kittens. After bathing and checking them for fleas, I could bring them into the house and provide them with a litter box. I could put a collar on the mom." Julie gently petted the bony mother. The cat turned her head and licked her hand.

"I'll get that food and be right back."

Julie found an old horse blanket and gingerly moved the family onto it. The mother never stopped purring. "I'll find you a spot in the house later. You're safe with me now."

The mother, who Julie named Minnie, gobbled the food Pearl provided, gulped the water, and rushed back to her babies.

"We did well today, including saving the kitty family. I left enough food to last a couple of days." Pearl wiped her hands on her jeans.

"Thank you. I'll go to the store tomorrow. Do you know if the tractor works?"

"It was running years ago. Tommy could come over to do maintenance and drain the fluids before starting it. Well, I should get home and make dinner. I expect to see you sitting at my table at six. Tommy will be there too. He's looking forward to catching up with you." Pearl gathered Julie into a hug.

"What can I bring?"

"Just you. See you then." Pearl waved, climbed into her yellow pickup, and drove off.

Julie had two hours until dinner. After dragging her luggage upstairs and putting her things away, she lay on her bed. She was soon fast asleep.

Surreal disorientation followed a restful sleep when she woke up in her old room. She could almost touch her past there. The sun was setting, and she had less than a half hour to get to the Rodgers'. She changed into clean jeans and a favorite white Gunne Sax blouse with puffy sleeves, ran a brush through her hair, and teased her bangs to give them some height. Just enough time to get the kitties food and water. She slipped her white-stockinged feet into clear jellies and was at the door when the phone rang.

She answered, believing it was Pearl.

"Hello, Miss Sandals, it's Doug Gober here. I'm calling to get your answer on that generous offer to buy your house and land."

It didn't make sense, but she decided right then what she wanted to do. "Yes, Mr. Gober. It was a good offer, but I'm going to decline. I'm going to keep the house and stay here."

There was a heavy pause. "Perhaps you require additional time for consideration. I promise you'll never get another offer like this one. Shall I come over tonight and review it with you?"

"No, thank you. There's no need for that. I am not selling, and I hate to cut you off, but I have dinner to attend."

"So, you're leaving right now?" Doug's voice had an uncomfortably high pitch. Maybe he was holding in hiccups or something.

"Yes, I am."

"Maybe you don't understand how good an offer this is." Disappointment tainted his voice, which had returned to normal.

"I should be going." Julie tapped her foot irritably.

"I imagine you're having dinner at the Rodgers' house. Are you positive you won't change your mind, Miss Sandals?"

"Yes, I am, and I'm running late. I'm positive I don't want to sell, just like my grandparents." Julie used a firmer tone.

He cleared his throat. "Okay, then. It looks like you've made up your mind. Enjoy your dinner, and say hello to the Rodgers for me. Please drive safely, Miss Sandals. Goodbye." Doug Gober hung up before she could respond.

She replaced the yellow dial phone on its cradle. Someday she'd get one of those new push-button ones. "Pesty man. No wonder Gramps had to kick him out. Must be a big commission for him."

Julie shook her head and left. This was a drive she hadn't made since the accident. Her headlights illuminated three small crosses with dried flowers on the right side of the Rodgers' driveway. She stopped in front of the crosses and threw the car into park.

"It will be seventeen years in four days." Memories from that Christmas morning tugged at her, and tears stung her eyes. She took a deep breath and pushed the emotions back inside, added some pink lipstick, and refluffed her bangs.

"I love you, Gramps and Grams."

Out of the corner of her eye, she saw someone standing next to a tree across the street, where the Rodgers' driveway lights only touched. She stared into the shadows as an icy hand from the past gripped her. No one was there. Why did that feel so familiar?

"Maybe a deer, Grams."

She hesitated to voice her suspicion of being observed from the shadows. That would make it too real. But why? People did take walks and didn't always want to chat. Even so, images flickered in her brain. The tree falling and . . . And what? Was there something she needed to remember? She scanned the area once more, saw only darkness.

"They must be wondering what I'm doing, Grams. I hope you and Gramps are happy in heaven."

Luckily no one was watching out the front window for her. Perhaps they understood what driving past where it happened would mean. She sighed loudly and drove onto the gravel driveway. To her left, an old stump marked the remains of the tree that altered her life.

She parked next to a yellow pickup and a black SUV under the large carport on the side of the woodshed. They used to park in the barn during winter, but it was farther away. The carport was close to the house, and no one had to see parked cars from inside. Soon she reached another familiar wooden front door, with a new wreath adorned with red bows and framed by glowing lights. Before she could knock, a tall, handsome man with golden brown eyes threw the door open, releasing a cinnamon-and-nutmeg Christmas aroma.

"Julie!" He pulled her into a hug.

"Tommy?" Julie didn't mind being in his arms.

"Yup, it's me. Guess I've grown a bit since you last saw me. I still remember you and Tessa following me around. I'm not the same grumpy big brother now." He laughed.

All the sadness disappeared as Julie grinned. "I'm not the same irritating little girl, either."

He stepped back and waved for her to enter. "I can see that. Please come in. Mom's been fussing in the kitchen since she came back. Wanted a proper welcome-home dinner."

With a gentle tug, Julie undid the buttons on her crimson coat. "Wasn't necessary."

Pearl called out. "It certainly was. This has been a long time coming. Offer her some wine, hot chocolate, or something, won't you, Tommy?"

"I will, Mom." He lowered his voice. "Here, let me take your coat. And so you know, she's the only one who calls me Tommy, since I'm the youngest boy. I go by Tom now."

Julie felt lost in his eyes. The crush she had on him as an eight-year-old hadn't gone away, but he probably was in a solid relationship by now. "Tom it is. A glass of water is fine. I don't drink much."

"How do you feel about sparkling water? We have lime and lemon." He hung her coat on the bare wooden coatrack that used to be covered in colorful scarves and coats years ago.

"Oh, my favorite. Lime, please."

"Lime it is. Make yourself at home. Mom just got a new leather couch. It's cold but comfy. I'll be right back." A momentary gaze, and time ceased to exist. Eleven-year-old Tommy would not have looked at her like that. Nope, that was new.

Julie felt like a schoolgirl as she sank into the brown leather couch. How many times had she and Tessa sat in here and played with their baby dolls or colored? The same painting of Lake Tahoe hung over the red brick fireplace, which was unexpectedly fire-free tonight. Needle-point Christmas stockings hung on it, with new names added to the family and one noticeably missing. The tall bookcase was filled with all the old classics, and the oak coffee table Tessa's dad had made was graced with a porcelain Santa and his reindeer-pulled sleigh. Another addition, a TV in the corner, replaced the old radio they used to listen to. She adjusted the bird pillow behind her back to study a full fir Christmas tree that added comfort to the room and gently held ornament memories and twinkling white lights. Colorful packages burst from underneath. Was this how the room had been decorated when she and Grams and Gramps had come for dinner? Not that it mattered what something looked like years ago. All she had was now.

"I miss you, Grams," she whispered. The star treetop took that moment to tilt sideways, like someone had bumped into it. A small pink bike, like the one she received from Santa years ago, swung back and forth. It was like—

Julie shot up and rubbed her arms. "Enough of that. Now I'm seeing things."

She turned and saw a group of family photos on the small table near the window. There was a picture of her and her grandparents. Her throat tightened as she studied the happy family in the photo. The hope in that little girl's eyes would soon be cruelly plucked away by an old oak tree. Out of the corner of her eye, she saw something move at the edge of the brightly lit driveway. She peered into the landscape as goose bumps covered her arms, but she saw nothing. Being here brought up her past. Yes, just her imagination.

Without another thought, she yanked the heavy burgundy drapes closed. Overstepping her visitor status? She was reaching to reopen them when Tom entered, carrying two glasses of sparkling water with a wedge of lime.

She held the small gasp inside. "I hope you don't mind—it's dark outside."

"Not at all. Saved me the trouble." He handed her a drink brimming with ice.

"Thank you. I thought—"

"Dinner!" Pearl called.

"You thought what?" Tom asked.

"Come on, you two, before it gets cold." Pearl peeked in.

"Be right there," Tom called to his mom. In a lower voice, he said to Julie, "You were saying?"

With great effort, Julie mustered a smile to hide her emotions. "Thought I saw something. Probably a deer."

Tom nodded but glanced back at the drapes with a frown.

The savory pot roast dinner was the best home cooking she'd had since she was a child. Julie kept eating her way past full. It was hard to get a word in edgewise when Pearl got talking. Tom's eyes were full of amusement as his mother talked and ate without pausing for breath. The love in their family was so apparent, and she'd forgotten what that was like. Julie was the most relaxed and happy she'd been in years sitting at the Rodgers' dinner table.

Underneath the good food, there was a strong undercurrent between her and Tom. But she'd only been in one proper relationship, and Brian had cheated on her twice, so her instincts weren't that great when it came to men. How stupid to give that guy a second chance. Plus, all the little loans he'd needed—well, huge lesson there.

Before she knew it, she had a large doggie bag full of pot roast, potatoes, and carrots to take home, along with a plate of chocolate chip cookies.

"Christmas Eve dinner is at seven, and you are more than welcome to spend the night here, Julie. Because we expect you here for Christmas Eve and morning," Pearl said.

"Thank you, if you sure I'm not imposing."

Pearl shook her head. "I thought we were past that."

Julie held up her hands. "Okay, I'll be here, but I'll sleep at home. You already have a full house. If you need some extra room, I have it."

"We can all fit. The ones that live close by stay home, but I expect everyone here by eight in the morning. The little ones are so impatient." Pearl grinned.

"I bet," Julie said.

"Mom's right. They rip through those presents. Anyway, I'll walk you out. I'm sure you want to get home. Maybe we could get some coffee on Thursday and catch up before the big family event. I know a place that makes the best pumpkin spice latte and hot chocolate."

Tom's mother pushed him aside as she gathered Julie in another hug.

Julie felt her cheeks redden as Pearl bobbed her head.

"That's a great idea, Tommy. Maybe Tessa can join you? She and Rusty are coming on that day, which is Christmas Eve. She has a surprise to share, and I have a feeling I know what it is."

"Oh, Mom. I know what you're hoping. We'll see." With a mischievous glint in his eye, he winked at Julie, causing her heart to skip a beat. "She told me she has last-minute shopping and wrapping, so she'll be busy, but Mom's right, she's eager to see you. I'll pick you up around five, if that's okay. Then we can head back here after." Tom opened the front door and grabbed the food from her.

"Yes. That works great. Thank you again for the delicious meal."

"Anytime, I mean it. Night!" Pearl called right before they stepped out into the cold together, leaving her standing in the doorway. They made small talk under Pearl's watchful eyes until they turned the corner out of sight.

Tom placed her food in the back seat, turned around, and pulled her into a hug. For a minute, she thought he was going to kiss her—unless this was the action of a guy hugging his little sister.

"See you in three days, Julie." He put his hands in the front pockets of his jeans.

"Thursday it is, but I was wondering, do you know Tessa's big surprise?"

"No. I know Mom hopes they're expecting. Tessa isn't letting on what it is, but Mom would love her baby to have one. That would leave me the only one without a family, and Mom is known for her match-making. I'm rooting for Tessa or Rusty to have either bought a house or gotten a promotion at that publishing house they work at. I'll let Tessa fill you in about her exciting life working with authors." Tom shook his head and held her gaze. "For me, it's important to find the right girl first."

Julie's cheeks felt hot, and she was glad for the shadows. Was he hinting, or was he one of those men who avoided that trip down the aisle? "Wow! Works with authors? I can't wait to see her." With a graceful movement, Julie slid into the car, settling herself comfortably in the seat.

"Well, see you Thursday." He shut her door and disappeared around the corner.

Julie started the orange Nova and cranked up the heater, which provided meager warmth. "A new car would be nice, but not if it means selling the house."

She sighed and pulled out of the parking place, waving once more to Pearl and Tom. The tree stump barely got a second glance. If it had been up to Julie, it would have been removed and replaced with flowers. Memories from that day were creeping in, and she was uncertain she wanted them. Her headlights brightened the area where she thought she'd seen someone, but no one was there.

She merged onto the two-lane highway and headed toward her grandparents'—no, her house now. The sharp corner that her grandfather had so carefully navigated that day was coming, and she pressed on her brakes, but they didn't respond. In a panic, she pulled the parking brake, but that did nothing. Her speed increased as she and the out-of-control car headed for the hairpin turn. She gripped the steering wheel tightly, hoping she wouldn't be killed in a car wreck like her parents and grandparents.

"It's a family curse," she moaned as the tires skidded on the asphalt. Fortunately, there was no ice or snow, only trees and a gentle slope off the road. She was doing forty-five, with a fifteen-mile-per-hour turn coming.

She did something she hadn't done since she was a little girl—she prayed. Her speed suddenly decreased as her car sputtered. Even if she turned off the road, the car wouldn't stop before she hit the trees.

The tires hit the dirt, and suddenly she was spinning. A tree was right in her path.

"Help me, please." She covered her face, waiting for the impact, but none came as the car shuddered and bumped its way to a complete stop in a patch of blackberries. Not only did she not hit the tree, but the car went around it, and the tangled brush stopped her from crashing into any other trees. She was alive. Grateful tears fell as the clouds lifted in her mind and she remembered what happened before she passed out seventeen years ago.

CHAPTER 4
1969, CHRISTMAS MORNING

THE TRUCK TIRES SQUEALED, her seat belt tightened, and it was hard to breathe. The decorated oak tree Julie had admired was falling, and they were in its path. As the tree hit the roof of their pickup, she yelled to her grandparents, but they didn't respond. Julie did what Grams taught her to do when she was scared—she prayed. But the prayer went unanswered as she was jolted back into the window.

She felt a sharp pain in her left side. A man wearing a long black coat and beanie paused near the truck. Why wasn't he helping? He glanced at her with the evil expression of the scariest monster in her worst nightmare. He held an axe and a red candle in his right hand, its wick unusually long. He smirked, lit the red candle, and inserted it deep into the broken tree trunk. He was racing away as Tessa's dad undid her seat belt. She strained to talk, but only groans came out. She passed out before she could warn him. If only . . .

CHAPTER 5
DECEMBER 1986

JULIE TREMBLED as though evil had touched her.

"How did I forget that?" She wrapped her arms around herself. "That wasn't an accident, Grams. A man held an axe and dynamite. I know him! We know him!" She took a deep breath. "Unless I'm imagining things, but unlikely. What are the chances that my brakes suddenly give out? It happened." She shook her head. "That face, those eyes. Pure evil! How would the police miss the difference between a tree falling and being cut and blown up?"

Julie shook her head and tried to start her car. Nothing. Her gauge always showed full, and she'd forgotten to keep track of how much gas she had. But would running out of gas slow her down? She was no mechanic, but it might, or maybe she was being watched over. It didn't matter. An urgency to get out of there pulsed through her. She swore she saw the white outline of a woman standing by the road. She rubbed her eyes, and the woman was gone, but her heart was racing, and every inch of her screamed *run*.

"Grams? No, can't be. But I need to get out of here and tell Pearl what I remember. This changes everything."

Julie grabbed her purse and jumped out of the car. She carefully made her way in the darkness toward the glow of the Rodgers' house.

It was her beacon of safety. Headlights sped in her direction, peeling out of the sharp turn. The vehicle was going way too fast, so Julie jumped off the road and used a large pine as protection in case the driver lost control. The car skidded to a stop where she'd crashed. Relief coursed through her as a flashlight examined the wreckage. She was about to call out when the driver threw a lit object that landed and rolled under her car. A cigarette?

"Hey, what are you doing?" It came out high-pitched and shrill, but it was unheard by the driver as the car's tires howled in a 180-degree turn. It sped down the strip of road, its red taillights fading around the sharp corner right as her car exploded.

Julie raced for the safety of the Rodgers'. Tom was already outside, running to the end of his driveway as she threw herself in his arms and explained what had happened.

He held her tightly. "Could be someone carelessly tossed out a cigarette, and you had a gas leak. *Could* have been going for help, I suppose."

"No. This was no coincidence. I had a flashback to when the oak tree fell on our truck." Julie rubbed her forehead.

"What did you see?" Tom's eyes narrowed as he held her protectively.

Tears ran down her face, and she gasped out the words that terrified her. "It was—" Two gunshots cut through the night.

Pain exploded in Julie's left arm, confirming that her memory had been real.

"Julie!" Tom tackled her to the ground. It knocked the breath out of her, and her arm felt like it was on fire.

"What's happening, Tommy?" Pearl's voice was filled with fear.

Tires peeled out, and the sound of a car speeding off gave Julie a bit of relief.

"Julie's been shot. Call nine-one-one and toss out the rifle, but don't come outside." Tom took control.

He rolled off and gingerly laid her flat, studied her arm, and then wrapped it in his scarf. "You're going to be okay. It looks like it went clean through. The other shot missed."

Julie finally got air back in her lungs and gasped in the welcomed, cool oxygen. Her mind cleared, but her arm throbbed like someone had tried to pull it off.

Pearl came out holding the rifle, her eyes scanning the road.

"Mom, go back inside."

Pearl shook her head. "You take care of Julie. I'll watch for our shooter until the sheriff gets here."

Tom sighed, pulled off his beanie, and tucked it under Julie's head. "Are you okay?"

She held up a hand. "Just my arm, and the breath was knocked out of me."

He pushed the hair out of her face and shook his head. "I'm so sorry. My only thought was to protect you."

Sirens could be heard echoing in the distance. Julie felt safe and cautiously sat up, keeping her arm still. She took a deep breath and put the puzzle pieces together. Tom took off his coat and wrapped it around her.

She leaned into him and started with what she remembered from the original crash. Pearl hovered over them. "It was no accident that oak fell. I saw who did it, Pearl. It was the same man Gramps kicked out. He and his son gave me an offer on the house, and I rejected it." Julie held Pearl's gaze as realization crossed over her face.

"Doug Gober?"

"Yes. He knew I was coming here tonight."

"I knew there was something wrong with him," Pearl mumbled, never taking her eyes off the road.

"You were right about him, Mom. It makes sense. You know his brother used to be the sheriff, right? Explains why they didn't believe us about an explosion."

Julie's eyes widened. "So you heard it? He isn't still on the force, is he?"

"We heard it. No, he retired or was forced out years ago. Never did like either of them, truthfully. But this?" Pearl's face was a mask of rage. "I worried when I saw he'd been to your house. He has a bad vibe, as your grandmother put it. He deserves to die for what he did to your family and ours."

Julie had never seen fury on Pearl's face before, but she fully understood it. She felt it too. "I agree, and there's more. I found something in the kitchen cabinet." She had their full attention as the red lights reflected off the trees. She should have given them this information earlier, but how could she have known she could trust them at first? The story of the gold flowed out of her.

"Now it all makes sense," Pearl said. She lowered the rifle, and her expression hardened as the sheriff's vehicle bounced into the driveway, followed by the paramedics.

Julie explained the situation to Deputy Collins before she was loaded into the ambulance, which she didn't want, but Tom insisted.

"You'll feed and check on the kitties, won't you?" Julie asked Pearl and Tom.

"Of course." Pearl's voice was pleasant, but her expression wasn't. Both women wanted justice.

The next few hours were a blur. Julie had never felt so tired in her life. Not only had she been shot, but a burden she'd carried deep inside had emerged. At least the bullet hadn't hit anything major, and the wound would heal soon. Strangely, it was the same arm she'd broken as a child.

Pearl and Tom picked her up from the hospital the next day.

"Before coming here, we did some shopping for you. You should be set for a while." Pearl's face was pale, and her eyes were red. Tom wore the same exhausted expression. It had been a long night.

"We have to make one stop at the police station. Their wish was to see all of us once you left the hospital." Tom helped her into his mother's pickup.

"Did they arrest him?" Julie asked.

"We don't know. They went quiet once they got all our statements. Sorry about your car. They said it was totaled, but they saw the brake lines had been cut." Tom's expression was full of concern.

"I needed a new car, anyway." Julie tried to laugh but didn't have the energy.

"They believe it was Doug Gober's doing," Tom added.

"Of course it was. Trying to finish what he started." Julie shuddered.

"But he didn't, and now he'll go to jail. I can't wait to see him behind bars and everything taken from him. He will pay for what he did to our families." Pearl sighed loudly and offered a tight smile. She pulled out of the hospital parking lot and headed to the sheriff's office. "You don't need to worry anymore, though, Julie. You can rest assured that you're safe now and he won't reach you again. You won't be alone until he's caught. Your car is totaled, but I still have the old Buick. Been sitting, but it runs. Borrow it until you can replace your car."

"Thanks, I appreciate that." Julie held back tears of gratitude.

"You're family, like I said," Pearl said firmly.

The brick building with ivy growing on the front looked the same as she remembered. They were seated in a small, newly painted white room with Deputy Collins. His scarred desk had silver tinsel taped to its edges and a small plastic tree to the side. The old-time Christmas music that Grams had so loved played in the background, at odds with the heavy mood.

The deputy was young, and Julie suspected he was new to the job. His light hair was styled in a military cut. Before speaking, he cleared his throat to catch everyone's attention.

"We spent all night searching for Doug Gober. His son didn't know where his father or mother was. I went to school with Doug Junior, and I believe he didn't know what his father was up to. During our expansion into different areas, a hunter reported a deceased man and woman found in the woods. Doug and Betty Gober. It appears to be a murder–suicide."

"So, he won't answer for his crimes and committed another murder on his wife," Pearl spat.

Deputy Collins looked down. "I'm afraid so. Sorry, Mrs. Rodger."

Julie gasped. "Mrs. Gober was the lady at the hospital following the accident. She kept grilling me on what I remembered."

"That's right. She worked at the hospital and was the person who kept me away from you, Julie. Guess she was no better than her husband. I won't feel sorry for her death." Pearl rolled her eyes.

"I can't say if she knew, Mrs. Rodger. At least we know the motive.

It was confirmed by old—I mean, retired—Sheriff Sam Gober. He confessed early this morning about a scheme to buy your land. They knew about the gold, Miss Sandals."

"So he admitted it? He was responsible for my grandparents' and Mr. Rodger's deaths?"

"No. Sheriff—Sam said he didn't know his little brother was behind their deaths. Doug convinced Sam that the truck exploded. It was never investigated past that, even though Sam had his suspicions. Doug insisted an inquiry would tie up the property for years. Not that it was true, mind you, but Sam foolishly trusted his brother, and it all got neatly buried. One thing Sam admitted to doing was tossing the guardianship papers and will they located at your grandparents' house. Thought it would be easier to get a hold of the land if you were in foster care. They figured eventually the property would have to be sold, and they'd buy it up."

"He tossed the papers and let poor Julie languish in foster care? He deserves to spend the rest of his life behind bars!" Pearl sat on the edge of her seat, staring down at the deputy.

"Yes, I wish that hadn't happened. At least the original will made it to the new law office before that fire. The rest, including the missing guardianship papers, must have been destroyed in the fire that killed Mr. Barnes, their lawyer. You remember? Bad wiring, although now I wonder. Mr. Barnes's partner, Mr. Keller, took over the executor's role and made sure the estate was looked after, but he didn't know about the guardianship papers, only the will."

"Jack and Margie always intended to redo their will and combine everything, but they informed us that we were named guardians. Said they'd get us a copy after the holidays. And yes, I remember the fire and poor Mr. Barnes's death. I wanted Julie but couldn't prove it was what her grandparents wanted. It was awful for all of us. If Sam had anything to do with that and Mr. Barnes's death, he should get the death penalty." Pearl shook her head and clenched her fists.

Deputy Collins nodded in acknowledgment. "That will all be investigated, I promise. Doug took the coward's way out. I hope knowing the truth brings you some closure, and at least Sam has been arrested and is sitting in a jail cell right now. Again, I'm very sorry our department was involved through Sam." Deputy Collins tugged at his shirt collar.

"I want to see him." Pearl stood.

Deputy Collins held up his hand. "He doesn't want visitors, but he wanted me to say he was sorry for his part. He killed no one and wasn't involved in the recent attempt to kill Julie. Sam cleared Doug Junior of any involvement too."

Pearl's eyes narrowed slightly with a hint of skepticism. "How can anyone believe him? I hope you throw the book at him."

Deputy Collins shook his head. "He's being transferred to another county per his lawyer's request, but that won't help him escape justice."

"Figures. Let's get out of here." Pearl stormed out of the room.

Julie stood with a grunt, and Tom rushed to her side. "If I had more energy, I'd storm out too."

Tom held the door that his mother had slammed. "At least we know the truth, and those who were involved aren't around us anymore."

"There's that."

"I'm sorry, and Merry Christmas, folks." Deputy Collins rushed past them like he had someplace to be, but Julie suspected he needed to get out of there. It was embarrassing for one of their own to be involved in a crime.

The ride home was silent until they pulled up to Julie's house.

Pearl turned off the truck engine. "You should stay with us until you're healed. Christmas is only a couple of days away, and the food we got you will keep. Bring Minnie and the kittens with you too."

"No, but thank you, Pearl. I need time to process and face things and get the house ready for Christmas. I won't let that man ruin another holiday for me. I feel like I've had closure and been given a second chance at life."

"Good for you, Julie. It might take me a while. I plan to be there during Sam Gober's trial, but for now, I want to focus on our reunion this Christmas." Pearl patted her shoulder.

"Thanks. I want the same, but I'm uncertain about attending the trial, if that's all right."

"You do what's best for you," Pearl said.

"I'm trying. You know, since I've been home, it's like Grams is with me. Maybe she's always been there. Maybe it was more than luck that I survived after Doug Gober tampered with my brakes." Julie blushed. The words seemed ridiculous when spoken aloud.

"I believe she is watching over you." Tom helped her out of the truck.

Pearl grabbed a bag from the bed. "I agree. She sure is, and she kept you safe. I'll put your groceries away and get the cats settled. They won't mind a bath if they dry by a nice warm fire. And don't say no. I honestly need to do something or I'll burst. Tommy can bring in wood and kindling. You can lift those pieces with one hand, right?"

"Yes, I can do most things without using that arm." Julie held up her right arm.

"I know you can, Julie." Pearl's face beamed with approval.

"How about I make us some coffee?" Tom said.

"Good idea, Tommy. But help her up the stairs. She should change out of those dirty clothes. That cute blouse is ruined and has blood on it. Sorry I forgot to bring fresh clothes to the hospital." Pearl shook her head.

"I'm fine, and I can manage the stairs, no problem. I'll be right back." Julie felt winded at the top of the stairs and grabbed some clothes from the closet.

With determination, she slowly changed, opting for a black T-shirt that fit loosely over her arm and a pair of sweatpants. The process took a lot longer than usual without a nurse's help. She only had to keep her arm still for a couple of days, so she would manage. After running a brush through her hair, she headed back downstairs to her guests.

Pearl raced around like a whirlwind and had the house in order within the hour. She wouldn't allow Julie to move from the couch, where she was covered by a snowflake-patterned fleece blanket and had a hot cup of coffee to sip. Tom had brought close to half a cord of wood into the house.

"I'm going to cut some kindling." He winked and disappeared outside with the old axe.

Pearl carried in Minnie and family, freshly washed, and set them on a blanket in a large box by the woodstove. "I dried them with the old hair dryer. I'll take them to our vet tomorrow and get them checked out. It'll be early. Do you mind if I let myself in and grab them?"

"Pearl, there's no need for you to go to that trouble," Julie said, "but please allow me to go with you."

Pearl pursed her lips and shook her head. "No. Your body has been through a lot. The doctor said a couple of days' rest was necessary."

Julie knew she wouldn't win this argument. "Okay, I'll rest. I don't mind you coming in, although I doubt I'll be sleeping."

"Never know." Pearl rushed back into the kitchen. By the aroma of tomato sauce that had overtaken the house, Julie knew there'd be pasta.

Tom brought in a load of kindling that would last her for several days. "You're set. I'll fill the kettle on the stove so the air doesn't dry out."

"Thanks, Tom. I hate sitting here feeling so helpless."

"There's nothing helpless about you. If I ever get shot, I'll let you bring in wood for me."

"Deal."

Pearl topped off Minnie's food bowl. "Okay, everything is done. I'll be back in the morning. Call me if you need anything. You're well stocked now, though."

"Thank you," Julie said.

"No thanks necessary. If you get lonely or need to talk, call. I'll be home through the New Year." Pearl gave the room a quick scan.

Julie's throat tightened as emotions threatened to overwhelm her. She hadn't felt this cared for since her grandparents died. After being enveloped in careful hugs, she was alone but didn't want to rest.

"Okay, Grams. This house needs some holiday touches."

The spare room upstairs held most of the holiday stuff: Gram's Santa collection, tinsel for the stair railing, candles, and a nativity scene that had been carefully put away by Pearl years ago. Julie took her time and transported the precious memories downstairs. She arranged the decorations in the exact way she remembered. Everything held good memories and pushed away all the bad she'd been through. She packed away the pictures, porcelain horse collection, and other small items in a box, which she discreetly shoved behind the couch with her foot, and added more wood to the fire.

"The only thing missing is a tree." A feather floated by and landed where the Christmas tree used to be. "I'll see what I can do, Grams." Julie yawned. Grams had told her more than once a floating feather meant an angel was near. The ghostly woman she had seen earlier— well, that was different. She stretched out on the couch and drifted to sleep.

When she awoke, it was dark outside, and Minnie was next to her, eyes reflecting the glowing light from the cracked woodstove door. Julie stood, and a pain shot down her arm. Time to take a painkiller. She flipped on the kitchen lights.

"Meow," Minnie said, standing over an empty bowl.

"I guess you're hungry."

After taking two pills, she grabbed a can of cat food. Once she got it on the electric can opener with one hand, it was simple. Minnie gobbled it down, used the box, and curled around her babies.

"My turn to eat."

She found spaghetti and sourdough bread waiting in the fridge in single portions to heat in the oven. Keeping her arm dry, she took a luxurious bubble bath while her dinner heated. The warm water almost lulled her into sleep, which could have gotten her arm wet. Shaking her head, she wrapped herself in a warm brown towel, put on the big T-shirt she loved to sleep in, and slipped into her comfy pink slippers. After gobbling the pasta and bread in the same enthusiastic manner as the hungry mother cat, she found room for two chocolate chip cookies. Yawning, she checked on the sleeping cats and climbed into bed, ready to read. Instead, unshed tears fell, releasing so many emotions and fears. After she blew her nose, she felt lighter than she had in years. Soon she was asleep.

. . .

When she woke, it was late morning, and her arm was now at a dull throb that she could tolerate for now. There was a note in the kitchen and a fresh Christmas tree.

Minnie and the kittens got a clean bill of health. The kittens are two weeks old. Dr. Frank suggested bringing them all back together in six weeks so they can get their shots. He recommended keeping them inside until that happens, just in case. I cleaned the box and rekindled the fire. Glad to see you sleeping, and the house looks great, but rest today, please. I moved that box upstairs and brought the rest of the holiday stuff down in case you don't listen and don't rest. I couldn't resist getting you a small tree. I put the lights on it because you need two hands for that. I hope you don't mind me taking over so much, but I think of you as one of my kids. Always have. Rest, and reach out if you require assistance.
     Love, Pearl

"Well, you got your tree, Grams."

Julie stood over Minnie and her babies. It was going to be hard to get rid of any of the three sweet kittens snuggled in a ball. After breakfast she put on Grams's favorite Christmas album, Bing Crosby's *White Christmas*, and decorated the tree, the holiday spirit taking hold like it used to when she was a child. None of the past events tainted her present moment.

She stood back and admired her little tree. "Perfect."

Next, she dove into holiday baking because Pearl had made sure she had the supplies to do so. It was a pleasant day filled with holiday cheer from her past, and she didn't give the man who ruined it all for her a second thought. He had done enough damage, and she wouldn't allow it to continue.

Finally it was Christmas Eve. Everyone was at church. She wasn't ready to embrace that, although it took some convincing for Pearl to accept it.

"I promise I'll go next Christmas Eve, Pearl. And I have all the food you brought over. I'm fine, just tired after getting shot. I'll rest and be ready for tomorrow." Julie felt bad using that as an excuse since it hadn't held her back the last couple of days, but there was something she needed to do—felt compelled to do. Go into her grandparents' room.

"I don't like you being alone, but you'll be ready bright and early tomorrow morning to get picked up by Tommy. Right?" It wasn't a question.

"Of course. I wouldn't miss it." It would be like so many years ago, but this time there would be no accident.

"Well, Merry Christmas Eve. If you change your mind about spending the night, call me."

"Honest, I'm fine. I need to feel close to my grandparents for tonight. Then I'll be ready to celebrate tomorrow. Merry Christmas Eve."

All the cookies and pumpkin bread she'd made as gifts were in old cookie tins she'd found in the Christmas decoration boxes. She wished she had more to give, but she couldn't drive a stick shift yet. Tom had helped her shop by picking up some wine and candy. It was the best she could do this year. The promised coffee date would have to wait until after Christmas—if it happened. They could catch up at his house too.

Julie sighed and headed up the stairs. She opened the door to her past. The room was just as she remembered, except the furniture was covered in sheets. She delicately pulled the sheets off the bed and sat on the familiar pastel quilt that Grams had made right after they got married.

"I can still smell your special floral scent, Grams, and Gramps's Old Spice that he loved. Can't believe it survived seventeen years."

She got to work. Despite her slow pace, she managed to clear out the drawers and closet, putting the contents into garbage bags for charity. What she couldn't donate, she'd have to throw away. It was like getting rid of her childhood.

"Sorry, Grams. It's time, though."

She dusted what she could and kept the farm pictures her mom had painted before she was born. On the top of the dresser were portraits of her family from when she was a baby. One was when she was two—the last time everyone was together. Grams's tortoiseshell brush—her gray hair still in it—and mirror were on the dresser. The black leather jewelry box contained Grams's and Gramps's wedding rings, her cross and emerald ring, and Gramps's tie clips that he rarely used.

Grams didn't like jewelry much and had never pierced her ears. Her mom's old costume jewelry was still in its wooden box. It was filled with the bright earrings her mother had so loved and her father's fancy silver belt buckles. Gramps's truck collection was in a glass cabinet, and at the bottom of that was their wedding picture. There weren't as many memories as Julie thought there would be, except on the top of the closet, where the photo albums and old letters were. This was what was left of her family—things she wouldn't let go of, ever.

A quick flash of bright light burst next to her and was gone as quickly as it came.

"Grams, is that you? I thought I saw you at the accident too."

Silence. Julie plopped on the bed and let the old tears run their course until they ran out. There were no other flashes.

"I'm okay now, Grams and Gramps." Julie blew her nose and sneezed again.

She hurried down the stairs and fed her sweet kitties.

"There you go, Minnie." She cleaned the cat box, tossed the bag in the trash, and washed her hands. "Time for my dinner. Wonder what's in the cabinet."

Pearl had left chicken noodle soup and split pea soup.

"I can carry on the tradition of soup, at least. Not the good stuff, but close." She ate her bowl of split pea soup and finished the sourdough bread while sitting next to the cats.

Minnie settled in next to her kittens and observed Julie.

"We'll have to come up with names for your babies soon."

Julie washed the dishes and then hung her stocking and left cookies out like she'd done many years ago.

"See you in the morning."

She fell fast asleep, feeling hopeful for the first time in years. She swore she heard her grandparents talking as she drifted off. At one point, it felt like her cheek was being kissed. Crazy dream.

The sunbeams reached in like hands between the drapes and woke her the way they used to years ago. She tugged the drapes open with the same enthusiasm. Blue skies greeted her over a surprise Christmas scene.

"It snowed last night. Perfect."

She put the final touches on her makeup and wrangled herself into a red sweater, the most festive thing she had, and a long black skirt. When she looked at her reflection, a smile formed on her face. Despite the car accident and gunshot, this was her happiest expression in years.

"Merry Christmas, Grams and Gramps." She glanced out the window, expecting to see Tom pull into the driveway, but was instead greeted with a rainbow, identical to the one that had welcomed her when she arrived.

"A rainbow over the snow? No coincidence—must be you, Grams. Thank you." About to leave, she noticed a penny on the floor that hadn't been there before. She tucked it into her skirt pocket. "No idea what I'm going to do yet about the gold. I could use extra money to update the house, fix things like the window, and get the apple orchard going again, but I don't want to tear up the land, either. I imagine that's what you would have done—mine on a small scale. I'm definitely staying put. I miss and love you, but you should move on if you're here. It's okay now that Doug Gober and his wife are dead."

A white feather floated by, and the rainbow disappeared into the gray skies. Love from the other side. Tom would be here any moment. She slipped into her fur-lined boots and rushed downstairs to greet him and feed Minnie. She was pulling on her grandma's wool cape— her coat was ruined—right as he knocked.

Opening the door, her heart skipped a beat. It had only been two days since she'd last seen him, and it felt like forever, as crazy as that sounded.

"You look beautiful, Julie. Merry Christmas. Sorry I've been so busy, but I got the items you requested. They're out in the truck. You ready?"

"Merry Christmas, Tom. I have a few gifts to add to what you got. Do you mind helping me carry them out?"

"Love to help. Did you change your mind about spending the night?"

"If you don't mind driving me back, I'd like to stay here and make sure the kitties get a Christmas treat."

"I don't mind at all." He held her gaze, and she felt a silly school-girl blush. He pulled her into a quick hug. Then he leaned back and caressed her cheek. "I hope I'm not reading this wrong, but I've wanted to kiss you since dinner that night—before it got crazy."

"You read it right." She smiled and tilted her head, inviting what she wanted.

He bent and brushed her lips with his. Gentle transformed into passionate, and the world faded away, just like in movies. The grandfather clock chimed twelve times. Breathless, she finally pulled away and rested her head on his shoulder.

Tom kissed the top of her head. "So much happened this week, but this makes up for everything. You know, even as a kid, I didn't dislike my little sister's best friend."

"Well, I didn't dislike you either, as the irritating big brother of my best friend. Should we go? I imagine everyone is waiting for us. And the kids are eager to open presents."

"Only after this." He pulled her into another kiss that she felt in her soul. Time disappeared as they melted into each other until the clock struck one and the kitchen cabinet popped open. They pulled apart.

Minnie peered into the kitchen and, with a swish of her tail, settled back with her babies.

Julie studied the clock. "I think Grams approves—well, unless she doesn't." The clock struck one again. "That a yes, Grams?"

The room was silent in anticipation until the chime echoed an answer.

"I guess I have your approval. Thank you, Mrs. Winsome," Tom said.

A flash of light lit the room for a split second as the outline of her grandmother appeared, exactly as Julie remembered her from that Christmas morning. With her thumb raised, she pointed at the clock. She headed for the bright light where her husband stood with his arms wide open, turned around one more time, and blew a kiss to Julie.

Julie's eyes brimmed with emotion as she blew a kiss back. "She's always been with me. I wish I'd known that in those foster homes. I wasn't alone after all."

Tom kissed the top of her head as the light slowly moved further away. "You weren't alone then and aren't now. We were visited by a ghost! A Christmas ghost. No one would believe us. I barely do, and I watched it happen." His voice was shaky.

Julie leaned her head on his shoulder. "We know what we saw."

He squeezed her good shoulder as they watched the glowing orb grow smaller and smaller until it was gone. Julie sighed, savoring Tom's arm wrapped around her. She was crazy about him and wished they could have stood there together the rest of the day. Ahead of her, a new life and relationship awaited. She regretfully moved away from him.

"You okay?" Tom asked, his face lined with concern.

"Perfect, actually. Don't we have people waiting for us?" She tilted her head.

"We do."

Julie grabbed her gloves from the table. "I have to repeat that last drive I took with my grandparents, now that the truth is revealed."

"If it's too difficult, I can remain here with you."

Julie shook her head. "No, I need to do this. Put the past in the past. If I was still in danger, Grams wouldn't have left, right?"

"No. She wouldn't have."

Julie followed him out into the wintry morning, ready to start living.

This Christmas morning, they pulled into the Rodgers' driveway without incident. Finally she got to celebrate in a house full of love and hope after seventeen dark years.

CHRISTMAS SHORT STORIES

CHRISTMAS REUNION

THE SHOPPING CART wheels pulled to the left, giving Zella Kellman a workout as she navigated the holiday merchandise. She heaved an enormous sigh of relief when she saw that the toy of the season, Beautiful Burping Baby, was still available on Christmas Eve. She snatched the last two dolls, one with golden hair and the other brown, and headed to checkout.

Zella felt a nudge. "Boy, you waited until the last moment."

She turned around to see a mature lady wearing a twinkling tree sweater and cradling a can of jellied cranberry sauce. She dug deep for some good cheer since, for the first time in years, she wasn't going to be alone. "Yes, well, last-minute travel plans to see family. Please, go ahead of me."

A smile smoothed the woman's wrinkles but not her arrogant tone. "Thank you for allowing me through, since *I* only have one item. Merry Christmas."

Zella stepped aside as the woman pushed past her with her one item that she treated like a brick of gold. That wobbly red log had always been on her dinner table as a child, but the oldest relatives were the only ones who ever ate it. "Merry Christmas."

After spending every penny she'd earned working overtime at the winery on her sister and the twins she'd never met, Aurora and Kahlan, Zella put the gifts in colorful holiday bags. She added sparkling tissue and placed them in the back seat with the snowman cookies and a bottle of zinfandel. Her tank was full, but she was starving. One more stop, and she had chicken strips, pumpkin-flavored coffee, and fries.

"Let's do this." Zella nibbled on her dinner as she merged onto the freeway.

The drive was effortless as she wove into the mountains where her sister and nieces lived. A place she hadn't been welcome to visit since confronting her ex-brother-in-law, Peter. She shuddered. How bad had it been for her sister and little nieces for the past four years?

Her favorite Christmas song came on the radio, and she crooned along out of tune. The car heater strained as the temperatures plummeted and ominous black clouds consumed the starry sky. "Please don't snow. I don't know how to put on snow chains."

Her request was denied as small flakes blanketed the black asphalt. A silver SUV sailed by in the fast lane, causing Zella to slow more. She clutched the steering wheel. She had to make it over the pass. Just had to.

She made it to the top of the summit without having to chain up.

"Downhill from here. Time for a pit stop." She pulled into the rest area.

Besides Zella, there was only a family with two little girls in matching snowman pajamas, snow boots, and heavy pink coats in the warm bathroom. After washing her hands, she checked her phone and found a text from Sue.

Please drive safely. It might snow.

She responded, hoping her message would get through with only one bar.

It's snowing. I'm at the Summit rest stop. Leaving now. Be there soon.

Zella grabbed more coffee from the vending machine and ventured back into the freezing night. Large snowflakes reflected the red warning lights from the highway with an eerie shimmer. Traffic halted, and a man emerged from his car.

There was an orange cone blocking the entrance to the road.

Zella let out a deep sigh. "An accident. If I hadn't stopped, I might have missed it—or been in it."

The family from the rest stop, already in their blue SUV, drove to the cone, where a highway patrol officer met them. The SUV backed up and parked next to Zella. Getting out, the father pulled on a black beanie that covered his windblown hair. He made eye contact. "Road's closed. We missed a huge accident ahead. Good thing we stopped."

Zella sipped her hot coffee. "I hope everyone is okay. Should be open soon, though, right?"

"The officer wasn't sure about the time line, but they need to get the injuries dealt with first and then move the vehicles. He suggested we wait inside, and he would filter as many as he could into the rest stop. Luckily, traffic is light right now, since most got over the mountain earlier." The man, who wasn't over thirty, pulled on black gloves.

"At least there's heating and a bathroom in the building."

"Yes, we're lucky to have that. See you inside." He assisted his pregnant wife out of the car. His young girls jumped out like they were on a great adventure. The family grabbed blankets and headed inside the gray cinderblock-and-wood building.

Zella reached into her pocket and pulled out her phone to check for any messages. There was no reply from her sister. She updated, assuring her she was safe and would be there soon.

She grabbed her cell phone charger and some cookies, determined to make the best of it. At least the people stranded here could celebrate. The rest stop had bathrooms, vending machines, and a small deck with a view of a frozen pond. It was surrounded by snow-clad pines. The room lacked seating, so she retrieved two folding chairs from under her suitcase in the trunk. Her sister had asked her to bring them. A maroon sedan pulled in, and an older man wearing a dark overcoat and cowboy hat nodded to her and hurried into the building.

Purse on shoulder, cookies in one hand, and the two folding chairs under the other arm, she pushed through the sideways snow. More lights flashed as emergency vehicles arrived. A family with a small crying child were making their way to the rest stop from the road. The mother carrying the child moved past her like she was a zombie and went into the building, but the father stopped and held the door open. He smiled weakly when she thanked him.

The mood had changed inside. The lightness she'd seen the children display was gone.

She opened the chairs and announced, "I have two chairs. I don't need them. Please, use them."

"I think the pregnant lady and the woman with the baby should use them," said the older man from the maroon sedan. He slowly unbuttoned his long black coat, exposing a red plaid shirt, jeans, and a large silver belt buckle with a longhorn on it.

"Thank you." The pregnant woman's face lit up.

"Yes, thank you." The woman with the toddler boy sat in the other with a loud sigh. He finally quieted and closed his eyes.

Zella smiled and asked in a hushed voice, trying not to wake the little boy. "I also have store-bought cookies if anyone is interested."

The girls looked at their mom, who said, "Go ahead, and thank you."

Luckily, she'd gotten the biggest tray they had at the store. The holiday sugar improved the room's gloom.

The young father who had held the door open for her spoke after he wiped cookie crumbs from his hands and glanced at his sleeping son. "We're lucky to be alive. We went between two cars that were spinning. Both hit trees, and one flipped. We plowed into a little white car pinned against a tree. I'm not sure if they—" He glanced at the children. "But we got lucky. They'll tow our car out of here, and I guess someone can come get us."

Zella spoke up. "I have room but no car seat."

He grinned, looking even younger. "Thank you. Ours is still intact. I wanted to get little Sammie and Carla inside. I'll return and retrieve the seat and our things. My name is Ken, by the way."

"Zella."

"I'm Dan, and I'll help you, Ken," the father with the two little girls offered.

The men walked off, and Carla, cradling her bundled child, whispered to Zella, "A man passed everyone and lost control. His car rolled and wedged against a tree. We hit that car. Not sure how we came out okay—all I could do was pray. I saw . . . well, some didn't make it."

Zella put her hand to her mouth. "That's horrible."

"Mommy? Can we open our gifts here?" the little blond girl asked, tugging on the pregnant mother's sleeve.

She pasted on a big smile. "It's not Christmas yet, Dina. But we have a veggie platter and chips and dip that Daddy can get when he's done helping that nice man. We can share, as Zella here did with her cookies."

Zella jumped up from the cool cement floor and tossed her empty coffee cup in the trash. "I can get them for you."

"Thank you. I don't want to keep walking on that slippery snow if I can help it. Being this pregnant brings with it a clumsy factor. We didn't lock it. It's in the back on a green platter, and the chips and dip are next to it."

"I can help, and so could Kellie!" Dina popped up.

"Please, Mom!" Kellie clapped her hands eagerly.

"Sorry, girls, but the answer is no. You want to get a peek at your presents. You stay here with me."

"I'll get it and be right back," Zella assured the antsy girls.

She shivered as the chill cut through her wool coat. This was not how she'd expected to spend her evening, but she had to go with it. She'd been doing that since the last time she'd seen her sister, when she told Peter to stop talking to Sue in that tone. If that was how Peter treated his wife in front of her sister, she couldn't imagine what he would do without her there. The worst part was that Sue had bowed her head and taken Peter's side obediently.

Later, she talked to Sue about going to a shelter.

Sue defended him. "He's genuinely good, just had a rough day."

All communication stopped after that genuinely *good* man texted Zella.

Leave MY wife and baby alone!

That was how Zella found out Sue was having a baby—or babies, as it turned out. No matter how many attempts she made to contact her sister, there was only silence. Until yesterday, when she got an unexpected call.

"Hi, Zella. This is Sue. Please don't hang up on me. I was terrible to you when you were protecting me. And trust me, I paid for that more than you know."

Zella's eyes filled with tears, and they streamed down her cheeks. "Sue! I'm grateful to hear your voice and know you're okay. I wanted to help you is all."

"I thought Peter would change, but he never did. It only got worse after I had twin girls. He wanted boys."

"I wish—" Zella couldn't get the words out.

"So do I, but I don't regret having my girls. Many times, I packed them up and was ready to leave. Peter would stop us with fake promises and then threats. Then a miracle happened—*Peter* left us! Said he was tired of always having to take care of us. Found out he got a girl pregnant, and she was having a boy. They moved away to be near her parents. Luckily, his family was never involved with us. I don't think they're much better than he is. At least he never hurt the girls. I'm grateful for that."

"He hurt you?" Zella gasped.

"Yes, but I healed."

"I'm so sorry, but I'm glad you're free of him." Zella had left unsaid her opinion that he should be in jail.

"The divorce is almost final. He told me if I didn't ask for money for the girls, he'd leave us alone."

Zella wiped her tears away. "I'm sorry, sis, he was pure evil. But I do feel for the girls."

"They didn't deserve a father like that, and I have a job and can support my girls without him. It's been sitting heavy on me—you're the only family we have. I threw it away for a horrible man. I did some dumb things, and letting him cut you out of my life was one of them. My only excuse is I wasn't thinking straight, only surviving. Can you forgive me?" The plea in her sister's voice broke Zella's heart.

"Without a doubt, I do. Can you forgive me for not helping you more?" Zella said.

"There was nothing you could do, trust me. I had two options: run away from him during his scarce work hours or wait for him to leave. And that's what he did. It was an answer to my prayers. I hope he doesn't treat the new girl the same way. I warned her, but she didn't listen, like me. I'm hoping we can put that all behind us and start over. Can you come here for Christmas? I mean, if you don't already have plans. This is kind of last-minute."

"No plans other than to watch old holiday movies and eat cookies. I'd love to."

"Hooray! I've missed you," Sue said.

At least that chapter was behind them. Zella carried the veggie platter and chips to her car, put it on the passenger seat, and moved the gifts to make room for the car seat and family. Maybe her sister's call was a sign that things needed to change. It wasn't like she made good money at the winery. She'd always meant to finish college and get a degree in computer science. She could work from home and live anywhere, even by her sister. Perhaps there was someone for her as well. All just a dream for now, though. At least the snow had slowed, and the flashing lights of the tow trucks and ambulances were like holiday decorations gone bad.

The men were soon at her car. "Put the car seat in here." Zella waved her hand. "There's space in the trunk for your luggage."

"This is so kind of you. I don't mind having the suitcases on my lap if they don't all fit," Ken said.

"I'll meet you both inside." Dan set two suitcases in the snowy asphalt.

"Thanks for your help, Dan!"

Sporting a friendly grin, Dan waved.

"We're going to Titus Valley to celebrate with the wife's brother. I hope that's not out of your way. I'm sure he'll come and get us no matter where you're going."

Zella said, "That's where I'm going too."

"What luck! Thanks again, Zella. The officer said they're trying to clear one lane to get us off the mountain tonight." Ken loaded the luggage into the trunk. Leaving room for the chairs, only one bag didn't fit.

"Good news."

The previously good-natured expression on Ken's face slowly disappeared. "The ambulance took away a pregnant woman, but her companion didn't survive. As she was passing on the gurney, the poor woman said something strange. Said her prayers were answered—she was free of Peter and he wouldn't take his daughters. She mentioned her failure to heed Sue's words. She must have been delirious. I hope she and the baby make it." Ken shook his head as he installed the car seat.

Zella let out a gasp of surprise. "It can't be. Are you sure?"

"Yes. Do you know them?" Ken stood and tugged on the seat, making sure it was secure.

"Peter is my sister Sue's soon-to-be-ex-husband. They have two girls. I wonder . . . You're sure he's dead?"

Ken put a hand on her shoulder. "I'm sorry, he is. I had no idea. I shouldn't have said anything."

With a gentle touch, Zella patted his hand. "I'm glad you did. He was a terrible person, and it would be a blessing if it was him."

Ken cleared his throat. "Uh. Well, that poor woman and baby."

A blush spread across Zella's face. "Oh, that was horrible of me to say, especially on Christmas Eve. I'm sorry. I hope the woman and her baby, as well as the others, are all right."

"Yes, I hope so too. Didn't look promising, but the night is full of miracles. I'll pray for those who passed and that woman and her baby." Ken added the suitcase to the back seat.

"I will too." Zella robotically rearranged the gifts so Ken or Carla could sit up front with her if they wanted to. Was Sue free of Peter?

After she locked the car, she followed Ken into the rest stop with the veggie platter, chips, and dip. The group almost completely wiped it out in half an hour. Dina and Kellie loved the ranch dip so much that they finished it with their fingers after the adults were done. Zella ate primarily for something to do.

Following an hour of pleasant chitchat, they resumed their travels. Zella dropped off the Newman family.

"Here's fifty dollars for gas. We appreciate you doing this for our family," Ken said.

Zella shook her head and pushed the money back into his hand. "Wasn't even out of my way. You keep it and do something fun with your beautiful family. Merry Christmas."

For a moment, Ken glanced at the money he held. "If you're sure. Thank you."

"Merry Christmas," Carla called, carrying Sammie still in his seat.

A handsome man stepped outside and scooped up the seat with the sleeping boy.

"That's Carla's brother, Jack. He opened a computer repair business in the old shoe store after serving in the navy for five years. He has a computer degree, like you said you wanted to get. Heck of a guy, and I hope he finds someone and settles down." Ken glanced at Zella. Was he match-making?

"Well, thank him for his service for me." Zella opened her trunk and caught Jack's blue eyes. He winked and headed in with his sister and nephew. She was glad it was dark, or her flushed face would have been obvious.

Ken was smiling as he scribbled a number on the back of a receipt for the veggie platter. He handed it to her. "If you ever need anything, call us. That's my cell phone number. We owe you. Merry Christmas, and drive safely, Zella."

"You owe me nothing. All I did was drive. My sister lives nearby, so it should be a safe drive. Merry Christmas." Zella stuffed the receipt into her pocket.

Ken gathered their luggage and headed to the house, which was adorned with vibrant decorations. With a last wave, they went inside. Jack peeked out the window and waved. Zella waved back, and the family disappeared behind closed drapes. Zella checked her phone and found a message from her sister.

You aren't going to believe this, but Peter died in the crash that held you up at the rest stop. Laney let me know. She and the baby are going to be okay.

Zella responded. *I wondered if it was him from a comment from the family I dropped off. I'm happy she and the baby are doing well, but I'm sorry for Aurora and Kahlan.*

Don't be sorry for them. Now we're safe, including Laney and her baby. She told me they were arguing. He turned violent, lost control of the SUV, and caused the accident. I shouldn't be relieved he's dead, but I am. Aurora and Kahlan won't sleep until they get to meet you. Don't mention this to them until after Christmas, okay? Drive safely. Love you.

Won't say a word. Be there soon, and love you too.

Zella hit send and bowed her head. Christmas prompted her to pray for Peter's peace and the happiness and healing of the innocent baby and mother.

She drove through the quaint town as the snow stopped. The snow chains that Ken had put on for her would have to come off later. Right now, she was enjoying the beauty. The clouds had cleared, and the stars shone like crystals in the sky. Life was precious, and it was time to make something more of hers. Her decision was made. She'd give her two-week notice after the holidays and find a job and apartment here. Maybe Jack would have a position for her at his computer repair shop, but a job at the grocery store would do while she finished college.

Zella grinned. Her heart was full when she pulled in front of the small house with a little Christmas tree in the window, glowing with joy. Her family was reunited and safe. This was the best gift she could ever receive.

A MAN AND HIS CAT

URSA DROPPED off his last passenger at her bus stop. He was off for the next week and looking forward to going home and watching football with his cat, Shoes. It wasn't everyone's idea of a great Christmas, but after his wife, Gloria, passed, it was what he had. They weren't blessed with kids to enjoy the day, but they always had each other, until last year. She had been his light and joy in a dreary world.

He worked diligently to provide for the cat his wife had adored. He had no desire to have friends and pushed concerned neighbors, coworkers, and distant family away. A few persisted for a couple of months and then honored his wishes. Alone, he could remember Gloria and pretend she was next to him, watching TV as Shoes lounged on his lap.

He entered the apartment carrying the old gal's special catnip treat. Shoes wasn't waiting for him in her box like she always did.

"Shoes?" he called. Nothing. He searched all her favorite spots. "Where are you? Are you resting in the shoes again?" He smiled, remembering how Gloria had named the small kitten who hid in their shoes. They planned to name her something else, but Shoes stuck.

Finally he found the cat, her orange tail draped over his wife's old sewing machine, which he couldn't bear to part with.

"You're missing her too, huh?" The cat lifted her head and sighed. "You okay?"

Shoes closed her eyes and went back to sleep. He felt the cat's hot nose. Shoes's breath came fast. "You aren't okay! I can't lose you too. I'm taking you to the vet. I don't care how old you are or how much it costs."

Ursa gathered the lethargic cat into his arms and tenderly placed her in the gray carrier. Without bothering to change out of his uniform, he tugged on the black wool coat Gloria had gotten him ten years ago, back when life was perfect, before lupus found its unwelcome way into their lives.

Grabbing his keys and the carrier, he stepped back into the freezing night.

"Merry Christmas!" his neighbor Bob called. "Going to visit family?"

"No. The vet," Ursa said. He got into the red SUV without another word.

He backed out of his driveway with Bob watching. "Hope Shoes is okay!"

Ursa waved and headed down the street to the freeway. It was a long half hour of listening to his lifeline struggle to breathe. He called to let them know he and Shoes were coming. Finally he arrived at the packed emergency pet hospital. Wide windows framed the concerned faces of owners. Not the place anyone wanted to spend Christmas Eve.

He rushed in with Shoes and filled out the required paperwork. He approached the tired receptionist, Sarah, who wore blinking deer antlers and a festive name tag. She took the clipboard from him. "Thank you. We'll get you in as soon as we can, Mr. Barber. It's a busy night."

"I'll wait in my car, Sarah. Don't want to stress her in here."

"Great. We'll come get you." Sarah nodded and answered the phone that hadn't stopped ringing since he walked in.

When he got back to the SUV, though, Shoes had stopped breathing. He pulled her out of the carrier, cuddled her against his chest, and rushed inside.

"Shoes isn't breathing." He softly pushed on her chest, hoping.

"I'll get Dr. James." Wide-eyed, Sarah jumped up and raced through the wooden door that led to the examination rooms.

She returned with Dr. James, who gathered Shoes in his arms and continued gentle compressions on the cat's chest.

"Let's get her into an exam room, Mr. Barber."

They entered a sterile white room with only a chair, a stainless steel examination table, and counters filled with instruments. In a haze of despair, Ursa heard Dr. James say what he already knew.

"There's nothing we can do for her. I'm sorry, Mr. Barber. When cats reach this age, the heart can fail unexpectedly. But I'm sure it was quick and painless for Shoes. There will be no charge for this." Dr. James gently laid the cat on the cold table.

Sarah covered Shoes with a small pink blanket. It appeared as if she was only sleeping, not dead.

"Thank you," Ursa mumbled.

The doctor put a gentle hand on his shoulder. "Would you like us to take care of Shoes for you?"

"No, no . . . I have it." Ursa scooped up the cat and headed back into the silent waiting room, where he felt sympathetic eyes on him.

He sighed and stepped out into the cold, tucking the pink blanket around Shoes. He gently placed her back into the carrier. "You're with Gloria now. What should I do without the both of you?"

He put on his seat belt and started the car. The heater roared on, but its warmth did little for him. Everything was locked inside him now, even the tears. Numb, he backed up and pulled across the street to a fast food drive-through. In the parking lot, he sat alone and nibbled on the burger and fries. He washed it all down with bitter coffee and headed toward the freeway. He went north, following Gloria's favorite star. It was the one she always looked for when they used to stargaze on hot summer nights. At that moment, a peaceful stillness enveloped him.

"I know what to do, Shoes. You should be buried where I spread Gloria's ashes. Yes, you'll like it there by the lake. It's so pretty. I still have the shovel in the trunk because Rob from work borrowed it last week, so I don't need to go home first." Ursa smiled for the first time since he'd bought a catnip toy as a Christmas gift yesterday. He'd bring that to Shoes on Christmas.

Soon he was at their spot. No one was there. He grabbed the shovel and pulled on his beanie and gloves. He carried the cat carrier with Shoes inside like it was a priceless Ming vase. She was that to him, and the carrier would be her protective tomb. It would keep her safe from any wild animals. The stars twinkled, but a bank of clouds threatened snow. He made his way to the bench he and Gloria always sat on.

Behind the bench was where he'd scattered his beloved, and now Shoes would join her. He sweated in the chill as he dug and dug. He scarcely noticed his arthritic hands. He was surprised the soil was so easy to work since the temperatures had dropped. Soon Shoes rested under the grand old cedar. He smoothed the ground.

"Can't even tell I've been digging here." Ursa wiped the dirt from his hands on his pants. "Sorry, Gloria. I'll wash them tonight."

Ursa wasn't sure how long he stood there, but the clouds were on top of him, and the first snowflake fell.

"I'll see you girls tomorrow. Merry Christmas."

Now every inch of him hurt, and the cold made it all worse. Still, he was happy he'd done it, even though it might not have been completely legal. The snow quietly fell as he put the shovel in the trunk. The burger and fries sat heavy, but he wouldn't mind another cup of coffee, or anything warm. He took a long, deep breath, peeled off his gloves and hat, and slid into the car. Turning the heater on high, he headed to the freeway. The hot air was blowing on him, but he wasn't getting warm, and his stomach hurt.

"Never should have had that greasy burger. Gonna make me sick, Gloria." He merged onto the highway, empty for once. The tears finally flowed, making it hard to see. He wiped them away and pushed them back inside until later. But they wouldn't be held in. A searing pain racked his chest. Nausea overwhelmed him.

"Oh!" He gasped for air. His exit was next, so he pulled off and stopped on the side of the highway to catch his breath, waiting for the pain to subside. It only increased. He reached for his cell phone to call for help.

His own voice was unrecognizable. "I'm Ursa Barber, in my car at the Golden exit. I need help. I'm in a—" Waves of pain crushed him, and the phone slipped out of his hand. He moaned as his head hit the steering wheel like a hammer, but the pain dissipated, and his breath came easier. "Whew, that was a close call. Guess I'm too old to dig holes at night." He laughed.

With each passing moment, the moon grew brighter, illuminating the night. The stars sparkled like diamonds, and he was no longer cold.

"Yes, that didn't help, dear." The sweet voice he remembered was by his ear.

"Gloria?"

"I'm here. I've always been here. It's time." She was next to him now and didn't look a day over thirty. His hand looked youthful, and there was no pain in his fingers.

"Am I dead?" Ursa reached for his beloved and felt her warm hand slip into his.

"I do so hate that word. We aren't dead, just in another form. You'll love it here, and you made it in time for the Christmas celebration. Here's Shoes." She tenderly scooped up the cat and cradled her with her free hand. The moon was as bright as the sun, and he had to squint.

"Are we going into that?" Ursa pointed.

"Of course."

"I've missed you," Ursa whispered.

"We will never be apart again. I love you."

"I love you too, Gloria. Well, let's go."

He held on to her hand and headed toward the light. He looked back at the elderly man in the car. That was behind him, and a whole new journey was in front of him and his wife. The best part was that Shoes was going along with them. This was going to be the best Christmas ever. His wife kissed his cheek, and they entered the light.

AT THE MALL

DESIREE WINSLOW SAT NEXT to the luminous tree that her family had decorated last week. The presents were wrapped in the blue-and-white snowflake paper her mother had gotten in the discount bin after last Christmas. Above the roaring fireplace, the chipped porcelain nativity scene was in its special spot. The windows were accentuated by the lighted garland, and snowmen of every shape and size were scattered throughout the house. The stockings were hung, and cookies and milk awaited Santa, but heavy fear and worry overrode the season's good cheer.

Even with her world turned upside down, Desiree was the oldest and understood what needed to happen for the magic to appear for her younger siblings. Ronnie and Sandra were already asleep, and her parents weren't coming home tonight. Her grandparents were sleeping in her parents' room. They had taken a red-eye flight and arrived a few hours ago. A quick nap was turning into a long night's sleep.

Desiree groaned and stroked their sweet lab's silky fur. His brown eyes understood her pain. "Let's get started, Sal."

He followed her up the stairs into the attic. The dim light cast dreary shadows over the memories, stories, and Santa's offerings. She gathered the gifts and carefully made her way back to the tree. Sal nudged her leg, and she presented him with an early gift, his bone from the North Pole. He settled onto his bed and savored it.

"Okay, let's get this done for Ronnie and Sandra."

Sal looked up.

"You'd help if you could, wouldn't you?" She patted his head, and he returned to gnawing on his bone.

Desiree choked down the cookies her mother had made a couple of days ago. She tried to drown her sorrow with the almond milk they all drank because Ronnie and her mom had a dairy allergy. She was used to it and didn't mind, but it didn't help.

Desiree's gift was the latest cell phone. She put it under the tree, but the gifts for her siblings would require assembly. She put the horrible situation out of her mind and focused on the job at task. "Who knew a doll's house would have so many stickers and this race set would be a pile of parts?"

Two hours later, she let out a boisterous yawn. It echoed in the house's holiday silence. She forced her tone to stay upbeat even though she was screaming inside. "Done!"

Sal sprang up like a jack-in-the-box and headed to the door.

"Okay, you do your business, and I'll throw the packing away."

Desiree filled a plastic bag and put it in the garbage can on the side of the house. She was finished with the Christmas Eve chores her parents had always done. Sal was at the back door. She let him in and shut off all the lights other than the ones on the tree. She settled onto the couch, covered herself with a fluffy snowman fleece blanket, and closed her eyes. Even though she was exhausted, sleep didn't come, but tears did. All she could think about were her parents at the mall, getting one more gift for the family. If only they had stayed home. Her life had changed a few hours ago.

The horrible scene replayed itself.

The first time she became aware of an active shooter at the mall was through her cell phone. She messaged her parents.

Are you okay? I saw on the news about a shooter.

We are hiding in the shoe store. We love you and your brother and sister more than life itself. If anything

The message cut off. Later, the doorbell rang. While Ronnie and

Sandra watched Christmas being saved on TV, Officer Andrew shared the news that someone had shot her parents.

The young officer had put a comforting hand on her shoulder. "The doctors are doing everything they can for them. I don't have any medical information other than they're both alive. Is there someone you can call to stay with you and your siblings, Miss Winslow?"

Desiree felt numb as she pushed her unruly, wavy brown hair behind her ears. She frowned and met the officer's pale blue gaze. "I can watch the twins until my grandparents get here."

"I'm sure a neighbor will stay with you until they arrive." Officer Andrew averted his gaze.

"Yes, don't worry, My brother, sister, and I have plenty of people to look after us. What hospital are they at? We should be there." Desiree grabbed her blue coat off the hall tree.

"How old are you?" His blue eyes narrowed.

"Sixteen."

"You can't drive your siblings, sorry. You need someone to drive you." He shook his head and studied the room before pulling a card out of his pocket.

She sighed and tossed the coat on the couch. "Yes, of course."

"Call this number if you need anything, Miss Winslow. Anytime. Someone will answer. And rest easy, the shooter is in custody and no longer a threat to anyone." Officer Andrew handed her the card and walked through the doorway.

Desiree stared at the blue-and-yellow card with an 800 number in her trembling hands. "Except those he shot."

"Pardon?" He spun around.

"I said thank you, Officer Andrew."

His freckled face reddened. "Yes, well, I'm praying for your parents and the others."

"Thank you." Desiree locked the door behind him. Only then did she let the tears flow, while her four-year-old siblings remained unaware. She firmed her shoulders, blew her nose, and called her grandparents.

"It will be okay, Desiree. We'll catch the next flight and be there soon. Love you." Her grandmother's voice quivered, and she hung up.

"We're hungry!" Ronnie came in, dragging his worn blue blanket with fire trucks on it.

Desiree hid her fears behind a stiff smile. "I'll make you some mac and cheese."

"Sandra wants marshmallows for dessert."

Desiree put her hands on her hips. "Sandra does, huh?"

Ronnie grinned. "We both do."

"Okay, if you don't give me any trouble. Is the movie still going?"

He wrapped the blanket around him like a cute superhero with curly brown hair, like hers and their mom's. "No, but there's another one to watch. Dad showed me how to start movies."

Desiree followed him into the room to make sure he could do it and found Sandra jumping on the couch, making her blond pigtails bounce.

"You know you aren't supposed to jump on the couch! Santa's watching," Desiree warned.

Sandra grinned and sat down with a dimpled smile that would melt anyone's heart. "Sorry. Don't tell Santa."

"I won't this time. Let me see you start the movie, Ronnie."

Without any assistance, her little brother managed it. Not trusting herself to speak as the tears threatened, she nodded at him. Would Dad teach Ronnie, Sandra, or her anything again? She took a deep breath as they settled in and headed back into the kitchen to get the water boiling for the pasta. While waiting, she tried the hospital.

"I'm sorry, we can't give out that information on the phone." The woman's tone was defensive, like she'd given this message more than once today.

"They're my parents." Desiree's voice trembled.

"I understand, honey. I'll investigate and call you back, okay?"

Desiree left her name and number but had little confidence in the nurse returning the call. Not with thirteen shot and ten dead. After Ronnie and Sandra were fed and happy, Desiree snuggled on the couch next to them but only stared at the TV, unable to process anything.

The phone rang, and she raced to answer.

Her grandma's voice had a forced cheerful tone. "Hi, sweetie. We're about to board our flight. I made a call to the hospital. Your parents are in surgery. They're critical but still alive. I made sure they would call when there was any information. They said it could be several hours before the surgeons are done. We should be there by then, and we'll stop by the hospital first. Okay, sweetie? You hang in there, and know we love you and your parents with all our hearts."

"I love you too." Desiree hung up the phone and finished watching the movie with her siblings. When the credits played, she stood.

"Time to get ready for bed. Santa can't come if you aren't sleeping."

"I want Mom and Dad to tuck me in." Sandra frowned as she pulled out her pigtails. Her hair stuck up like she was standing in the wind.

"They're running late." Desiree abruptly changed the subject. "Plus, when you get up, Grandma and Grandpa will be here."

"Yay!" Ronnie jumped around like a rabbit.

"I thought they weren't coming until after Christmas cause Grandma had to sing in church." Sandra crossed her arms and folded them tightly across her chest.

"She found someone else to take her place," Desiree lied. She wouldn't tell them what happened until she knew whether their parents would be okay.

After showering, brushing their teeth, and making sure the cookies and milk were out, Desiree read "'Twas the Night before Christmas" to them. Finally their sweet brown eyes were shut in sleep.

The phone rang again, and Desiree anxiously answered it, hoping for good news. It was her grandmother. "We saw them both, sweetie. The surgery went well, but it will be a long night for everyone. Let's remain hopeful that they'll wake up soon. We're on our way there." Desiree read between her words—the outlook was grim.

She had cuddled with the dog by the Christmas tree, clinging to elusive hope. Her grandparents arrived fifteen minutes later.

"We're gonna take a quick nap. You get some rest too, sweetheart."

While her siblings and grandparents slept, Desiree prepared the house for Christmas morning, no matter what the outcome. She sank into the couch by the tree and let her emotions flow, clinging to Sal. She blew her nose and sighed audibly. Sal licked her cheek and jumped off the couch to chew on his bone.

"At least they're both alive, Sal. Now we need a Christmas miracle. Please don't take them from us. We need them. Heal them, please," she whispered, worrying that only the dog heard her request.

She blinked and rubbed her eyes when the star at the top of the tree flashed brightly like a searchlight for several seconds, then dimmed to its normal glimmer like nothing had happened. Was that a good sign? She prayed it was. Just as she dozed off, the phone rang. Her grandmother answered.

"Yes, it is. What? Both? Are you sure? Thank you."

"What is it, Bea?" Her grandfather's voice was groggy.

"Oh, Bob! You won't believe it. They both woke up at the same time. Their vitals are normal, and they're clear-headed. It was like . . . " Her grandmother was crying.

"A miracle?" her grandfather said.

There was a loud intake of breath, and her grandmother cleared her throat. "What we prayed for. See, the doctors were wrong. They said they wouldn't survive the night."

In the early dawn of Christmas, Desiree raced into her parents' room and threw herself into the comforting arms of her grandparents.

"They're going to be okay, Desiree. The doctor said they were both asking for you kids. We'll see them in a couple of hours. It's the best Christmas present I've ever received."

"Me too, Grandma."

"You're all grown up, but when you were little, you always climbed into bed with us when you spent the night. Even at sixteen, you're still welcome. Grandpa will prepare for the kids."

"Yes, I'm on it." He jumped up.

"I took care of that, and I'm not too old, either," Desiree added.

"Well, it's almost six thirty, and I'm wide awake. I'll make coffee and pancakes while you girls get more rest." He shuffled out of the room.

With her grandma's arms wrapped around her, Desiree fell into a peaceful sleep she'd never felt before, one that only miracles left behind.

MIRACLE IN THE ER

DANIELLE REYNOLDS SIGHED and hit the buy button. She had to choose between getting her kids Christmas presents and paying bills, and one more month couldn't hurt with the bills. She'd take extra shifts, but her five- and six-year-old girls only had a limited amount of time to enjoy the Christmas magic. PJs, a doll each, and the dollhouse, books, and new outfits wiped out her checking account.

She shivered and wrapped an old fleece blanket around her. It was expensive to refill their propane tank, so they saved what little they had left for quick showers. The girls pretended they were camping and set up a blanket tent. They had adjusted better than she had to their daddy starting a new family with the neighborhood single mom, who had no issues with a man being already married. Luckily, the happy couple had moved three hours away for a new job. Through neighborhood gossip, she learned that they were already expecting their second child.

"Mac and cheese for dinner, girls?" Danielle peeked into their space.

"You aren't supposed to look, Mommy! We're doing some important stuff for Christmas. But yes to mac and cheese." Yvette pursed her lips together, crossed her arms, and narrowed the dark, heavy-lashed brown eyes she had inherited from her father.

Danielle let the flap drop. "Sorry. Carry on. I'll make us dinner."

"Do we still have chocolate pudding, Mommy?" Kyla peeked out. Her blue eyes shone like a summer sky. The complete opposite of her confident older sister, she was a clone of Danielle, down to her straw-berry-blond hair and quiet temperament.

"We sure do."

"I hope they have more at that food place for us. I like it." Kyla clasped her hands together.

Danielle was grateful that they had food to eat. "Tomorrow, I'll visit the food bank. I'll let them know how much you like it."

"Good. I'm going to tell Santa how nice they are to us. Thanks, Mommy."

Danielle held back tears as she entered the kitchen. At least they still had power—until the day after Christmas, anyway. She'd already had to shut off the cable and her cell phone. They were behind on the Wi-Fi bill, and that shutoff date was tomorrow. But at least she was current with her house payment, so they had a place to live, without power or heat.

Dennis had given her the house—and the huge mortgage payment —with the stipulation that he wouldn't be paying any spousal or child support. His expensive lawyer wove his way around the divorce like a python, squeezing any reason out of it. With no money to fight him, she gave in to the demands. This lawyer made sure she understood that if in the future, she changed her mind and wanted child support, she'd owe Dennis half the value of the house and back rent, and it would be sold. An empty threat since she was paying the full mort-gage and there was no equity in the house, but she gave in, glad the girls could stay in the only home they knew.

She thought she'd found the man of her dreams. Granted, they had only dated for six months, but he said he was happy that she was preg-nant. She dropped out of school a semester before graduation, and they eloped by beautiful Lake Tahoe. They came back and bought a house that he wanted to put in her name. What appeared to be a romantic gesture of love wasn't. It just made it easy for him to leave, and under California law, he still owned half. After three years of marriage, she found out the man she loved didn't feel the same way about her or the girls. He insisted he had tried, but she wasn't the one for him. After the papers were signed, he didn't try to contact her or his children. He had a new life with the real love of his life. The girls had stopped asking about him.

"Boy, was I stupid," Danielle mumbled as she added powdered cheese to the drained noodles.

She'd switched to the night shift at the hospital to get higher pay, lucky her best friend would spend the night with the girls. It left little time for sleeping, but at least she was working.

Kyla and Yvette's burst of giggles pulled her out of her poor-me mood.

"Go ahead, Dennis, and raise your shiny new kids in that rich family you married into. You don't know what you're missing with your girls."

"What, Mommy? Is dinner ready?" Yvette called.

"It sure is. Go wash, girls."

Dinner flew by, and the girls were finally in bed. A soft knock at the door signaled her departure.

"You look so tired, Danielle!" Vicki pulled her into a fierce hug. "I have tomorrow off. I'm gonna hang out with the girls so you can sleep in."

Danielle shook her head. "I'll be fine. You already do too much for us."

Vicki pulled back and pursed her full lips. "Rubbish. I like to see my goddaughters awake occasionally. I insist."

"I want to take them to Santa tomorrow."

Vicki offered a half grin as her brown eyes flashed. "We can go after lunch. Santa is there all day."

"I hope they don't ask for much." Danielle shook her head. "I did what I could."

Vicki shut the door behind her. "They're smart girls. There's no need to worry about it. All they want are fashion dolls and books. I can help with that."

"I got them—and the house." Danielle forced a smile.

"How?" Vicki placed her hands on the generous hips that always caught men's attention.

"Don't ask."

"At least you still have power, and I can give you enough to catch you up on that bill tomorrow when I get paid. Call it my deposit. Once I move in, things will get better—you'll see. I only have one more month on my lease. Then you got yourself a roommate. Just like old times." Vicki winked, a mischievous glimmer in her eye.

"Except for all the partying."

Vicki laughed. "No. We'll still have parties, but they'll be with dolls. Look at us, two single ladies who picked the wrong guys. At least you got two beautiful girls and a house out of it. I got my car and half my overspending ex's debt. Fun stuff."

"Yeah, who knew we'd end up like this?"

"What, two stunning women any good man would be lucky to have? And who wouldn't want to help raise your beauties?" Vicki's optimistic attitude matched her "bottled sunshine" hair, as she called it.

Danielle tightly embraced her closest friend and held on to her for a moment. "I hope to meet this alleged good man. I'd better go, or I'll be late. Thanks again, and love you!"

Danielle rushed out into the cold to catch the bus. Her shiny new minivan had been the first thing to go. The temperature outdoors wasn't much different than inside her house. If only she'd been able to buy wood for the fireplace, that would have helped. If only she had finished nursing school, she'd have RN pay instead of a CNA check. She might have money for cable, heat, and groceries. So many if onlys.

The night passed quickly. The ER was filled with car accidents and the flu. When she could catch her breath, she gulped warm coffee to stifle the yawns. The hospital had one of the biggest emergency departments in the area and was always busy. She had an hour left when a frantic couple raced in holding a limp child. Dennis's limp child.

Terri's belly was enormous, and she appeared close to her due date. She pleaded with Angelia at the front desk. "We're visiting my parents from out of town. He was fine when we left but got a fever tonight and started shaking. It wouldn't stop, and when it did, we couldn't wake him. We should have called nine-one-one, but my mom said we could drive here faster. Help us."

Ted and Dave carefully took the small boy, who bore a resemblance to her older daughter, and wheeled him away with the parents following. They didn't notice her; she wanted to leave before they did.

"I need to stay at the desk, Danielle. Can you get that couple's insurance information? I didn't want to hold them back," Angelia said, sorting through a pile of papers.

Danielle sighed. "Isn't there someone else? That's my ex-husband."

That pulled Angelia's attention away from her stack of papers. "Oh, I didn't know. If you watch the desk, I'll go do it."

"Thank you, Angelia." She sat in the chair with a sigh of relief.

She registered an older man who was coughing. By the sound of it, he needed x-rays. She moved him up the list.

Morning was arriving in a rosy glow right as Santa entered the ER carrying a huge toy bag. The jolly man dressed in red exclaimed, "Ho, ho, ho! Special delivery for the kids!"

Angelia came back with her clipboard. She grinned. "Thanks, Santa. If you could put them behind my desk, we'll make sure they get to the kids later. Unless you want to come back and hand them out?"

The man, who sported a real white beard and twinkling blue eyes, was the perfect Santa. "Wish I could. But I have North Pole stuff to deal with. You understand."

"I do." Angelia winked at Danielle as she peered inside the bag. Security would go through it next.

He directed his attention to Danielle. "You've been a good girl this year, along with your beautiful daughters. I made sure everything is taken care of for you. Don't worry, Danielle. Merry Christmas!"

The expression on her face turned into a frown. "Um, sure, thanks. Merry Christmas." She glanced at Angelia after he waved and exited the building. "How did he know I have daughters?"

"Must have been a patient, and you probably told him. Sometimes they like to come back and play Santa because their lives were saved here." Angelia grinned.

"I don't recognize him." Danielle studied the large figure retreating into the parking lot.

Angelia shrugged and glanced at the clock. "He was wearing a beard and padded red suit. Hard to tell who was under that."

"That beard looked real, and that wasn't padding," Danielle said.

"Well, so many go through. Hard to remember them all. You're almost off, but it would be helpful if you could check in one more patient and assist with their room assignment. You could avoid your ex." Angelia held up a finger, pushed back the red hair that always wiggled out of her ponytail, and picked up the persistent ringing phone.

Danielle checked the list of patients waiting and reached into her front smock pocket for a mint.

"What the—" She pulled out a thick envelope with her name on it.

Stuffed inside was a banded stack of hundred-dollar bills that had to be ten thousand and a note.

Danielle,

This should help pay for propane and those outstanding bills. There's a spot for you in nursing school next semester. It's fully funded by the North Pole scholarship, along with living expenses. Just one semester left—you can do it. Thank you for your kindness when people needed it.

Merry Christmas,

Santa

"I—" She tucked the money back into the envelope with the note and carefully placed it in her pocket.

That money was a miracle! She'd been praying for that exact amount—what she needed to catch up. She had told no one, not even Vicki. She took a deep breath and felt a heavy burden lift. With a burst of energy, she attended to the older man who was coughing, and even though it was the end of her shift, she made an extra stop to ensure her girls' half brother was okay.

Joshua, his eyes wide open and a bright smile on his face, was fully awake. Another miracle happened that night when her ex-husband apologized to her and asked to see the girls before they went home. Forgiveness filled the ER the night Santa visited and left magic behind. Now Danielle was a believer.

WORDS HURT

SALLY MACNEI DECORATED the white-lit faux tree with blue ornaments while listening to her favorite Christmas album. She found comfort in savoring her hot chocolate topped with marshmallows from a Santa face mug decorated with sparkles. Nevertheless, no matter how festive she made it, the holiday season was destined to be anything but normal. Not after what had happened at her sister's Thanksgiving table.

She sighed, finished her beverage, and wiped her mouth with the back of her hand like her niece, Maggie, did. Maggie was the only person she missed, but she'd make it up to her if they let her.

"I sent Maggie the gifts, anyway. Plus, I'm sure that family we adopted this year will enjoy the little extra gifts we sent them, right, Ellie?"

The little dog peeked from behind the Christmas tree. She blinked her gentle brown eyes and settled in for a nap like a fluffy snowflake. "Glad you agree. Don't knock anything off the tree," she cautioned the impeccably groomed bichon frise with the fake diamond collar.

Sally placed the blue snowflake gift bag full of new squeaky toys for Ellie under the tree. That bag wouldn't make it until morning. Her coworkers had given her gifts, but the absence of the presents she had bought for her family made the tree feel incomplete.

Although it wasn't her fault, she'd make the best of it. Being alone had its benefits, like eating whatever she wanted. She was looking forward to the organic Christmas feast for two she'd pick up later. It came with a turkey breast, mashed potatoes, and gravy. She'd skipped the green beans and gone with double stuffing and real wheat rolls. The dessert was her favorite apple pie instead of traditional pumpkin. She planned on lots of leftovers.

"It will be fun, Ellie."

The dog's ears perked, but she didn't open her eyes.

"After dinner we can watch all the sappy holiday movies we want. Perfect day, if you ask me."

She pushed down the thought that "sad" might be a more accurate description. But after those harsh words between her and her sister, Tracy, there was no going back. Her mother promptly took Tracy's side, as usual, and Sally was okay with that, wasn't she? After all, Sally was the vice president of an advertising firm, with a sought-after corner office, and until last week, she'd had a brilliant boyfriend.

"Rick, ha! The power couple—what a joke. Hope that frumpy secretary is ready to be his mommy, because that's what he needs." She had canceled his cigar-of-the-month membership and returned the new golf clubs she'd gotten him.

Her pocket vibrated, letting her know she was getting a call. She let it go to voice mail. "I understand your expectations, Mom, but I am not going to apologize in this situation. Good try. Bet you heard about the breakup. Well, that changes nothing."

The oven timer went off. "Sheet cake is ready!"

See if Tracy could make one like hers. Probably burned it, like she did that one year. Sally's turned out perfect. The perfection extended even to the sprinkles on top.

"Everything is *so perfect*." Sally covered the dessert, fed the dog, and slipped into her wool coat and cashmere gloves. "I'll be right back, Ellie. I'm gonna get tomorrow's dinner before it's too late."

The elevator ride felt never-ending, with holiday cheer playing in the background and a lingering scent of expensive perfumes. The specialty market was only a block away, so Sally walked. She smiled. She could enjoy her meal without concern for Rick's dairy allergy or her sister's celiac issues. Just plain, normal food.

"Happy holidays, ma'am," Dean the cashier greeted her as she entered.

"Yes, right, thanks, Dean. Same to you." She ignored the carefully placed holiday tip jar like she'd done all season. Wasn't up to her to make sure the employees got a decent wage, was it? After all, she gave a poor family new coats and socks, and her niece got the latest video game. She'd done her part and was being more than generous. As a bonus, she could write most of it off on her taxes.

On the way back, she grabbed a taxi—no use in dragging the food home through the crowds. Another person waiting for that extra holiday tip didn't get it from her.

"Enjoy your abundant holidays, miss."

"You too." Sally, in the holiday spirit, ignored his sarcastic tone.

She offered a nod but no tip for her doorman and soon had her dinner put away for Christmas.

After a rapid trip to the animal area, where Ellie did her business promptly to get back into the warmth, she wagged her tail expectantly by her empty food bowls.

"Someone is ready for their Christmas Eve dinner."

Sally scooped Ellie's meal out of the plastic container in the refrigerator. The turkey meal reminded her of chunky baby food, but the dog loved it. Ellie gobbled it down in a few bites and, with a loud sigh, plopped next to the Christmas tree.

Sally was interrupted once more by the buzzing of her cell phone. Her mother. "Boy, she doesn't give up." Had she forgotten that Tracy suggested that her then-boyfriend wasn't a good match? Practically came out and said he was too good for Sally. Rick had stood and grabbed their coats. Things would be very different if they had left instead of saying what she did. Since that day, the moment kept replaying in her head.

She had flung her turkey-printed paper napkin on the table and ignored the offered coat. "Who are *you* to judge our relationship? At least *I* didn't have a child with a deadbeat who's now in jail. And look at you. You can't even support your daughter. Mom helps you all the time. Keep your opinions to yourself, because I certainly don't need them." She snatched her wool coat and tugged it on.

Tracy's face paled. "I only meant—"

Their mother had jumped right in. "Maggie, why don't you go into your room and get that book you were telling me about? I'll be right there." As soon as Maggie was gone, her mother's eyes narrowed. "That was uncalled for, Sally, and especially in front of Maggie. All your sister did was point out what we've all observed." Extending her arm, she softly patted Tracy's hand as a gesture of reassurance.

"Of course you'd protect her, Mom, and to suggest I meant to hurt Maggie . . . " Sally shook her head and sighed. "Maggie knows her dad is a loser. All I was doing was being honest and protecting Rick. You're lucky to have each other, because I'm done with this."

Tracy called out, "Wait, Sally. This is a big mis—"

The door slammed behind Sally, cutting off the rest of the sentence. It had been a muted drive home as she felt the disappointment ooze off Rick even after she'd defended him.

Sally smoothed her hair and silenced her phone. "What's done is done." She opened a can of tomato soup and poured it into a saucepan. She slipped into her special Christmas PJs while the soup heated. After making a tray with her soup and fresh sourdough bread from the bakery across the street, she headed into her bedroom and slipped into her new flannel sheets. Plain gray for her and Rick. At least they were soft, but not like the charming Charlie Brown sheets her sister and mom had gotten her a few years back. She had tossed them out last Christmas because they were wearing out.

She flipped on the TV and streamed her favorite movie, *It's a Wonderful Life*. She gobbled up the tasty bread and emptied her bowl.

A glance at her phone showed persistence. "Seven missed calls? Give up, Mom. You defended Tracy, remember? Just like you always do. I'm the one who went to college and has a successful career. But you have no problem with Tracy telling Rick to leave me. Miss Single Mom who can't even buy the dinner she cooks. Yep, that's all on you, Mom. You babied her, and now look. She works two jobs and can barely pay rent, and my poor niece has no father. Great job. Well, Tracy,

I let you know what a loser you are." Sally's face reddened with her choice of words. Ellie let out a loud sigh. Even the dog was ill at ease. "'Loser' might have been harsh, but she was out of line."

Sally went back to her movie and was asleep when someone banged on her door. She threw on her bathrobe and opened it, expecting it to be more cookies from a neighbor, but it was Rick, dressed in a suit and wearing a sour expression. She rubbed the sleep from her eyes. "What are you doing here?"

"If you'd answer your phone, I wouldn't have had to stop by on the way to my parents'. I owed your mother at least that." Rick stood with his arms folded across his chest.

"My mother called you?"

"Yes. She didn't know we ended it."

"I'm sure Mom was happy to hear about our breakup." Sally rolled her eyes.

"No, she wasn't. But I don't want to argue. Your mother has been trying to contact you. Your sister was in an accident and is in the hospital."

Sally's mouth fell open. "I . . . she . . . it can't be."

"Get dressed, and I'll take you."

Sally mechanically switched off the tree lights. "I don't need a ride. I can grab a taxi."

Rick shook his head. "I'm going there to make sure that Tracy is okay and you get there. Let's go."

Sally picked up her purse but set it down. "I can't go. She wouldn't want to see me. I'm sure she'll be fine."

"I don't know why I care so much, but I do. You're going, and I'm taking you. Your family *needs* you." Rick bent to pet Ellie, who demanded his attention.

Sally opened her mouth and then shut it. She stomped out of the room and pulled on jeans, a white sweater, and leather boots. She threw her hair into a ponytail and applied lipstick. That would have to do. Besides, her sister was likely faking it to get her to come. And the nerve of this man to insist she go with him. Her anger flowed into worry. What if it wasn't a ploy by her sister and she was really hurt?

Her hand trembling slightly, she reached for her phone and dialed her mother's number.

"Sally! Where have you been? I've been calling you for hours."

"Sorry, Mom, but my phone was on silent. *Rick* showed up at my door, thanks to you."

"There's no time for that now. It's Tracy. They don't think she'll make it through the night—" A sob ended her mother's rant.

Sally gasped. "What? No! What hospital?"

"Mercy General."

"I'm on my way." She grabbed her purse and coat and followed Rick out the door.

It was a silent drive as she replayed all the unkind words she'd thrown at her sister. Tracy might have hit on some truths, but there was equal truth in what Sally had said. And all of it would have been better left unsaid that night. Now she might lose the one person who was always there for her when their parents divorced, their dad moved to another country, and their mother worked long hours at the law firm. Sally had erected an immense wall to protect that scared little girl, but Tracy had always understood. Had been there. What if their final words were spoken in anger?

"She can't die."

Rick glanced over at her and patted her shoulder. "She's a fighter, Sally."

Those built-up tears burst through the wall. Tears from when she was strong for her mom after her dad left them. Tears from watching her sister struggle after dating a con artist who, when he found out she was pregnant, left her with nothing. Tears from holding on to Rick and pushing him away at the same time so he wouldn't hurt her. Tears from never hanging on to any friends other than coworkers, for her cruel words to her sister in front of Maggie. So many tears that she'd held inside for too many years. The wall collapsed, and perfect Sally was a perfect mess.

Rick handed her a napkin, and she blew her nose. "Sorry."

"No, don't be. I wish I'd seen your emotions before. I knew they were in there. I didn't know how to reach them."

Sally sniffled. "Well, you've moved on."

Rick stopped at the red light, a sad frown on his face. "But I haven't. Not sure where you got that idea."

"I saw you hugging her. Your secretary." Sally observed her immaculate manicure.

"Connie? She got engaged. I was congratulating her." The light turned green, and Rick shook his head.

"Well, oh. I'm sorry. I've never said that, but I am. I've mistreated everyone because I was afraid of being hurt. There, happy? I'm a mess too." Sally wiped her eyes and looked out the window. The joyful decorations and lights held no meaning as they sped by.

Rick turned the corner into the hospital parking lot. "Not happy to see you in pain, but I'm relieved you realize it. Please tell your sister this too."

"What if she won't listen? Or what if she can't hear me?" Sally took a deep breath.

He reached out and grasped her hand. "Say it anyway."

Sally rushed into the hospital with a tiny bit of hope while Rick parked his car. She ran straight into her mother's arms.

Her mother squeezed her tightly. "She's in surgery still, Sally. I haven't heard anything."

Sally felt like a little girl being comforted by her mother's hug. "I'm sorry, Mom. Really, I am. I've been horrible."

Her mother pulled away and locked her eyes on Sally's. "Thank you for saying that. But neither your sister nor I have ever given up on you. We both still love you. I want you to know that."

Sally was consumed by shame, and she wallowed in a deep despair. In a quiet voice, she asked, "Where's Maggie?"

"With the neighbors. It's going to be a long night, and I didn't want her . . . well, I don't know." Tears welled up in her mother's eyes.

Rick walked in and pulled her mother into a hug.

"Thank you, Rick."

"You're . . . " His voice faded away as a nurse approached them.

"The doctor wants to speak with you now."

"So she's alive?" Her mother's voice was full of hope.

The nurse avoided eye contact. "The doctor knows more. Follow me."

The young doctor had dark circles under his eyes. He spoke in a gentle tone. "We repaired what we could and stopped the bleeding. If she makes it through the night, she stands a better chance for survival. She's healthy and young, and you can go in and see her for a bit, but please don't stay too long. She needs rest above all. There are vending machines with hot coffee and a chapel down the hall."

Her mother gasped, and Sally spoke. "Thank you, Doctor. Can you tell me what her injuries are?"

"You are?" He glanced at her mother, who nodded.

"Her sister."

"Well, a broken femur I repaired, a burst spleen that was removed, and some internal bleeding that was the priority. Her skull was cracked, and she suffered a severe concussion, which is now our biggest concern. Plus, there are many bruises, but fortunately, nothing else was broken. She's the sole survivor of the accident."

"So there's a chance?"

"There's always a chance as long as she's breathing. I'll check back in a few hours. She's in the room right there." He pointed. "She won't be awake, though, for several hours."

They entered the darkened room. Monitors beeped in a soothing rhythm. Their mother rushed to Tracy's bed and grabbed her hand. "We're here for you, honey. Don't give up. Fight for Maggie." She kissed her daughter tenderly, stood, and smoothed her hair. "Buy me a cup of coffee, Rick?"

"Sure." He squeezed Sally's shoulder and walked out with her mom. Sally sank into the chair next to her battered and bruised sister, to whom life had been exceptionally cruel.

"Tracy? Can you hear me? It's me, Sally."

She took a deep breath and held her sister's hand like their mother had. "I'm sorry, sis. I've been an idiot and afraid. To protect myself, I treated Rick, Mom, and especially you badly. I'm the worst sister ever and said horrible things, so I doubt you'll forgive me, but still, here I am. I showed courage by crying in the car on my way here. I have to admit you were absolutely correct. I shut down and tried to become this perfect person. But it wasn't me. You're the best of mothers and sisters, trust me. You were brave enough to choose to have Maggie, and you've raised her so well. So fight, sis. For Maggie, like Mom said. The thought of losing you is something I cannot bear. After all, it's Christmas, and I'm expecting a miracle."

She squeezed her sister's hand, brought it to her cheek, and kissed it. "They say I can't stay long, but I'm not going anywhere. And I'm going to turn over a new leaf, like the guy in my favorite movie. You know which one. This was my wake-up call."

"Sally . . . " Her sister squeezed her hand back.

"Tracy, you're awake!" She leaned in and kissed her cheek.

Tracy's voice was barely above a whisper. Sally had to strain to hear her. "I heard everything. It's okay. You're my sister—there's nothing to forgive. I love you and hope you can forgive me."

"Of course I do, and I love you too."

Tracy gasped and spoke in a softer voice that made Sally lean closer. "Please, take care of Maggie."

"Of course I'll take care of Maggie until you get better." Sally patted her hand.

Tracy breathed in deeply and exhaled slowly. "If I don't . . . promise you'll raise her."

"I promise, but it's going to be okay. You'll see." Sally let the tears fall.

"Thank you, Sally." Tracy's pained expression faded into contentment.

"Now get better. It's a good sign that you're awake. They fixed you." Sally was full of hope.

"An angel is standing right next to you. You're never alone." Tracy pointed with the hand attached to an IV.

"What? Really? Cool. She's here for you, though." Sally looked behind her but saw nothing.

"Love you and . . . " Tracy started.

"Love you too."

Her sister drifted back into sleep, the monitor displaying she was still alive. It was going to be okay. Sally was convinced.

But Tracy wasn't okay, and that was the last time she saw her sister alive. The angel took her when Sally went to tell her mom and Rick her sister was awake. Although they had made their peace, Sally knew she had failed Tracy so many times. She planned to make it up, starting with raising Maggie and taking care of their mom.

That Christmas may have been the saddest of her life, but it was the one that made Sally into the person Tracy knew she could be. Sally could get through anything with Tracy watching over her—as the angel she always was.

THE CHRISTMAS EVE WALK

THE HOUSE WAS DEEP-CLEANED, the decorations were up, and presents had been mailed to her sister. Linda Jones glanced out the window at the neighborhood's festive glow. There was magic in the air tonight—that was what her mother used to tell her and her sister. If she had a wish, what would it be? The man of her dreams? He definitely hadn't been Curt.

"Well, can't hurt. I wish for my soulmate to find me under the Christmas Eve star I can't see." Linda grinned, proud of how well the holiday season was going, especially after the unexpected breakup. A familiar bolt of anger coursed through her like a bad burger. After all, she had expected him to propose, not end it.

"Nope. Not going there," Linda informed her current best friend and furry companion, Bubbles. The shepherd mix had belonged to her sister until she moved out of the country to start over after her husband moved on from her. Must be a sibling thing, Linda thought. So she had inherited the poorly named dog, who she now called Bubs.

A beep came from her phone. A text from Curt.

I hate to bother you, Linda, but I believe I left snow boots at your house. On my way to Tahoe and hoping you are home so I can swing by and pick them up.

Without thinking, she responded.

I'll be here.

She stomped off, Bubs following close behind. "Can you believe him? Some wish that was, and now he's on the trip *we* were supposed to take. They've only been officially dating for six weeks, Bubs. We were together for two years. I had to earn my vacation with him, and that woman gets to go right away. Maybe she's paying for it, because he sure never wanted to part with his money."

Bubs sighed and sank onto his bed.

Linda quickly located the black size 10 men's boots in her coat closet, glad to get them out of her house. Curt wore them the first year they were together when they went to cut a Christmas tree. The tree that she paid for had ended up at his house.

His smooth explanation had overridden her concerns. "Makes sense it's at my house, hon. I mean, my family is coming, so it would get the most use here. Although my family would love to meet you, I won't stand in the way of you seeing your sister for Christmas."

She should have paid attention to how hopeful he appeared right before he hid a smile behind pursed lips. No, she'd focused on the beautiful blue eyes that always mesmerized her, missing the hint that he didn't want her to meet his family.

"I mentioned going to Mexico, but I hadn't planned on it this year."

"No, you go have fun with Elizabeth—I insist. My family will be disappointed, but they look forward to meeting you in Lake Tahoe next year, when everyone will be there." Curt patted her head like she was Bubs.

"If you think I should."

"I do." Curt nodded decisively.

So she'd bought the plane ticket, boarded Bubs because Curt's mom was uncomfortable around dogs, and headed south. She had a beautiful tropical Christmas with her sister involving many margaritas, but she missed the snow. She spent the next several months dreaming of Tahoe and the possibilities. She concluded there was a proposal involved after Curt invited Elizabeth to join them, but that all changed two weeks before Halloween via text.

My family can't make it to Tahoe this year. It would be better if Elizabeth came next time. You understand, don't you, hon? Just the two of us. It will be great. My treat.

Linda understood a week later via another text.

I think we should shelve our Tahoe trip, Linda. I'm going to spend the holidays with my family. It would be good to take some time apart and see where we stand in the New Year.

"See where we stand"? A fancy way to say "see ya." To confirm that, right before Thanksgiving, Linda saw a new woman draped on his arm like an old blanket at the mall. At least he looked uncomfortable before she went in the opposite direction. Then came the next text.

I'm sorry, Linda. I met someone. I hope you understand I didn't mean to hurt you.

She opened the door to a frigid blast of air that gripped her. His familiar black Chevy SUV pulled to the curb, and next to him, fixing her makeup in the passenger seat, was that woman—Missy. She was a cheerleader for the 49ers, and her dad was loaded from selling his startup in Silicon Valley. No wonder Curt had chosen her. With a satisfied smirk, Linda dropped the boots on the front porch, slammed the door, and locked it.

"Thank you! Merry Christmas, Linda!" Curt yelled through the door.

She peeked through the hole but didn't reply. He offered a slight wave and raced down the steps toward his dream girl, who was pumped with injections. Yes, her cheap lawyer ex had moved up in the world—or down, if you asked her sister Elizabeth.

Her phone buzzed with another text. Against her better judgment, she opened the message.

I had hoped to talk to you in person, but I wanted to be the first to tell you that Missy and I are getting married in Tahoe this week. Know we only wish the very best for you and hope you meet the right person too. Merry Christmas.

"He sure didn't waste any time. Bet she's pregnant."

It would serve Curt right. He'd wanted to wait several years to have kids. Mr. Split-the-Cost of Everything, who preferred to let her pay because he had student loans and couldn't afford any new debt. She should have seen the signs sooner—he wasn't as into her as she romanticized he was. Linda turned her phone off and left it on the table in case he had more to say. She pulled on her warm down coat, leashed up Bubs, and headed outside to clear her head.

Stepping through the trees and onto the familiar trail, she felt some of the tension float away right as the first snowflakes of the season landed on the brown leaves and pine cones. The sting of his marriage didn't hurt as much as it should have. Instead, it was kind of a relief. She almost laughed picturing his worried expression. Maybe the man felt a sliver of guilt for making her a placeholder. The reality was he wasn't her soulmate, and it was more her pride that had been hurt than her heart. Elizabeth had repeatedly pointed out their lack of compatibility. Although he had ticked several boxes—handsome, successful, and they both liked hiking in nature—that was where it ended.

Someday she'd thank Missy. The cheerleader had done her a favor. Bubs happily trotted next to her, stopping to smell or mark his territory. Linda's shoulders relaxed as peace crept in. The last bit of anger faded away, and she was ready for new adventures.

"Hello! Anybody there?" a youthful male voice called, startling her out of her musings.

"Yes! Do you need help?" Linda shouted.

"Yes!"

"Coming!" She wasn't worried that it might be a trap or a crime waiting to happen. In that moment, her maternal instincts took over. Plus, Bubs's tail was wagging. She wholeheartedly trusted her dog's instincts. He had always avoided Curt. Bubs tugged on his green leash, pulling her toward the voice.

Linda found a boy of about ten or eleven sitting on a rock holding a small black kitten. "Did you find that?"

He nodded, his curly brown hair bouncing around a thin face.

She stooped. "It's so tiny! I have a scarf we can wrap it in."

"A scarf works. Can you hold this kitten while I get the rest of them and the mom? With this storm coming, it'll be too cold for them to survive. I wasn't sure if I'd be able to get them all back to my brother's house by myself. Thanks." He tenderly gave her the kitten.

"I'm here to help." She unwound her pink scarf and wrapped the tiny kitten, who offered no resistance other than a weak meow.

Bubs sniffed the scarf and snorted.

The young boy narrowed his piercing brown eyes. "Your dog won't hurt the kitten, will he?"

"No, he's a sweetheart. He loves our neighbor's cat. Best friends." Linda held the little ball of fluff close to her to keep it warm.

After one more glance at Bubs, the boy turned his attention back to a log pile. "I heard its meow when I was out walking. I can see there's more in there. There's—oh, no!"

"What?"

"Only one other kitten is warm. The mother and the other two kittens are . . . well, they aren't alive."

"Here, let me see." Linda slipped the wrapped kitten into her pocket, pulled her glove off, and reached inside. He was right—they were gone, but the white kitten nudged her hand. She grabbed it and handed it to the boy. She searched the old stump for any more signs of life.

"Thanks. We should bury the mother and other babies." The boy frowned.

Linda shook her head. "Later. Right now, these babies need help. I'll call my vet."

He held up his hand. "My brother is a vet. He just moved to the area. Can I use your phone? My brother's house is a couple of blocks away."

"I left my cell phone at home, but my house is right over there." Linda pointed. She felt around in the hole in the tree stump once more. Nothing. "My name is Linda, by the way. Do you live with your brother, or are you visiting?"

"Paul. And yes. Our parents died a few years ago. The kittens should stay together." He handed her the even tinier white kitten.

"I'm sorry."

Paul shrugged without further comment. Linda put the white kitten with its sibling in the knitted scarf. They jogged off with Bubs in the lead. At home Linda turned on her phone and was relieved not to see any new messages from Curt. She dialed the number Paul provided for his brother's office.

"Four Paws."

After the receptionist heard about the two kittens, she put Linda on hold and promptly returned. "Doctor said to bring them both in immediately. Thinks they'll need antibiotics and milk."

"I'll bring his brother, Paul, with me too."

A second of silence passed before the receptionist replied. "His brother? I . . . sure. Well, we close in an hour, so you might want to hurry."

Linda disconnected and placed the kittens in a box with a fleece blanket. "She sure acted weird when I mentioned you. Not a fan?"

He grinned but remained silent. His clothes looked dated, as if he was wearing hand-me-downs. Maybe he was. Something felt off, but what? He seemed to be a sweet and caring boy, but she wasn't the best judge of character, evidenced by Curt. Maybe he was a brat.

Linda checked the dog bowls, washed her hands, and turned down the heater. "All right. Let's go."

Paul followed her out to the car. He was soon wearing a seat belt and holding the box with the tiny kittens on his lap. "My brother would like to meet you. He never gets out to meet new people. He works too much and needs to socialize."

Was the kid trying to set them up? Well, as late in the day as it was on Christmas Eve, it was probably a good thing his vet brother was available to see the kittens. She doubted her vet would still be around, and it might have meant a long drive to the emergency pet hospital. It was lucky the boy had found the kittens—she doubted they would have survived the night.

Paul caressed the two small kittens and barely answered any of her questions. They arrived at a wood-shingled building she passed every day. She parked and grabbed her purse. Paul handed her the kittens but didn't move.

"Aren't you coming in with me?" she asked.

"No, I want to go across the street and get a cherry cola slushie. Tell him that for me, and that I told you about him. Honestly, he's the best and needs a soulmate. Tell him all of that. Promise?" It was clear from his expression that he was being serious.

This day was getting stranger and stranger. No more making wishes. She couldn't wait to tell Elizabeth about it. "Of course, I'll tell him, I promise." Linda grinned at his match-making attempt. "You have money?"

"Sure do." He trotted off and disappeared into the store.

She rushed in with the kittens and filled out some papers.

The receptionist had a forced smile. "The doctor is ready for you."

"Thank you. Paul's getting a slushie. He should be here soon."

"Paul? Okay." Her tone turned frosty. "Well, I'll be here." Her focus was on her computer screen. She said nothing else.

"Yes, he wanted—" Linda was interrupted by the most handsome man she'd ever seen. Dark brown eyes and wavy black hair like his little brother, and he was movie star good-looking.

"Bring them in, Miss . . . ?"

"Call me Linda, and you must be Paul's brother."

A scowl crossed his face and disappeared when he glanced at his receptionist. "I am. Call me Dave. Let's examine the kittens you discovered."

Linda handed over the two tiny kittens. He carefully inspected them without saying a word. It felt weird to blurt out his brother's message and obvious setup.

"Are they going to be okay?" Linda asked instead.

"Let me run a couple of tests. We'll be right back." He opened the door and shut it behind him. The seriousness on his handsome face was evident. She hoped they would survive.

Dave's voice carried into the room where she was waiting. "How could she know him?"

Linda couldn't hear the answer. Big brother must not like his little brother talking to strangers. That made sense. Never know nowadays. She would explain it to him when he came back. Time passed much more slowly in that tiny room decorated with animal artwork, including dancing cats and dogs. She sat and waited.

Dave finally returned and cleared his throat. "With the mother and the other kittens dead, I can only assume they need antibiotics. I took some blood but won't have results for a couple of days. So we can keep them here, start them on medicine, and get them to the shelter—unless you're willing to take care of them?"

Linda stood. "Yes, I'll care for them. And I apologize. I didn't tell you when we first met that your little brother, Paul, found them. He wanted me to tell you he's over at the market getting a cherry cola slushie. He insisted I say you need a soulmate. Sorry, I think he was match-making. Sweet kid, though—looks like you. Sorry about your parents."

Dave's face turned a pale shade that didn't suit him. He sank into a chair and shook his head. "Paul died in that car accident with my parents years ago. You must be mistaken."

Linda experienced a tightening sensation in her throat and struggled to speak. That explained the receptionist's cool demeanor. "I—maybe someone played a prank on me. I'm so sorry. I had no idea. That's a cruel trick. I apologize."

"Maybe not so cruel." Dave rose and gestured out the window. "Do you see what I'm seeing?"

Paul was standing there, holding a cup and sipping from a red straw. With a wave, he vanished.

"He's gone, but—" Linda was unable to finish.

Dave shook his head. "It doesn't make sense, but that was a ghost."

"Like the Ghost of Christmas Past?" Linda couldn't hide the skepticism in her voice.

"Maybe. Only Paul would know his favorite slushie flavor, and our mom always hoped I'd find that soulmate. There was a big age gap between us, and I wasn't living at home when a drunk driver hit them head-on. There were no survivors." He rubbed his temples.

"I'm sorry you lost your family to a drunk driver, but I'm not sure I believe in ghosts." Linda stared at the spot where the boy had just been and studied the landscape for a camera. "This isn't funny if it's a joke."

Dave frowned deeply. "I would never play a joke involving my little brother. I loved him and my parents." He wiped a tear away and pulled a picture out of his wallet.

Linda's face reddened as she studied the picture in her hand. "I'm sorry. I didn't mean . . . "

"Check the date on the back." He pointed.

"Oh, my. Ten years ago, but this is the same boy I just spent time with, even wearing the same outfit." Linda's hand shook as she handed the picture back.

"I can understand your disbelief, and I'm trying to make sense of it, but that was my brother, Paul. I'll get the antibiotics and milk and make sure Cindy prints out your care instructions." Dave stepped around the metal examination table and, in three large strides, was out of the room.

A strong feeling of guilt washed over Linda. It was obvious he loved his family and was hurting. She had to allow that she'd been with a ghost.

Dave quickly returned and handed her the canned milk and liquid antibiotics for the kittens. "Here are the instructions. I'll want to see them after Christmas. Schedule the appointment with Cindy."

"I will." Linda blurted, "Dave, do you have plans for tonight? You know, a place to go?"

He turned and shook his head. "No, I was going to catch up on my reading. Have had little reason to celebrate the holidays since the accident."

"I find myself alone this year after a breakup and would like the company," she offered. She instantly wanted to take it all back and sink into the nearest hole.

"It appears that both of you are currently unattached. He'll be there," Cindy called. "I saw him too. He came back to bring the two of you together. Don't mess it up, hear me?"

Dave shrugged. "I guess dinner it is, if you're sure."

"I'm sure, unless you don't want to?" This level of boldness was unusual for Linda. Could ghosts urge you to say things?

"He wants to!" Cindy yelled.

His face turned red. "She's right. What can I bring?"

Linda couldn't help but break into a joyful grin. "I was going to make lasagna, and I have plenty of sweets and a nice bottle of wine I splurged on. You don't need to bring a thing. My sister, Elizabeth, is in Mexico, and I didn't have the funds to visit her again this year after repairing my roof, so it's just me. I work at the accounting firm in town. Well, you don't need my life story, so how about, welcome to our town?"

"Only been here a few weeks. Cindy came with me from the city. Thought it would be good to start over. Let's get those babies home. Would you like to join us, Cindy? If that's okay?" He smiled.

"Of course," Linda said.

"No, not me. I already have friends from the church. Got my whole Christmas planned out, and yes, he was invited but declined. You two get to know each other. I have a good feeling about this." Cindy grabbed her purse and sauntered out. "Merry Christmas."

"Merry Christmas. Follow me," Linda said, hoping she wasn't making a huge mistake. But what was the big deal in making a new friend, a ridiculously handsome new friend? She felt that tiny spark inside, and when he handed her the kittens, electricity passed between them. His astonished expression said it all.

A ghost had answered her Christmas wish. Linda couldn't wait to call Elizabeth tomorrow.

THE RED TRUCK

THE CHRISTMAS SEASON had stretched out to a luxurious three weeks of anticipation on Verna's calendar. But with each breath, time raced forward, and now it was Christmas Eve. Although gifts had been bought, decorations were up, and plans had been made—it felt incomplete. There was so much joy to capture and imitate from the movies she'd watched over and over. Verna sighed. Her life wasn't a movie; she had obligations to fulfill and a job that canceled whatever precious moments she grasped. Plus, there were bills to pay since she'd overspent on gifts for family, friends, and charity.

She set the red coffee mug with Santa's smiling face on it in the sink. "It's time to go to work. Make sure our town gets their daily caffeine."

Her decade-old black cat, Johnny, opened bright green eyes and swished his long tail. She petted the hefty cat's head, and he cringed at having his fur ruffled.

"I'll miss you, Johnny, but you know our favorite neighbor, Sam, will be feeding you dinner—and, I imagine, a couple of treats too." She slipped into her long, fluffy green coat and locked the door behind her. She tugged on her hat and gloves and pushed the elevator button. The old doors crept open like they would prefer no more guests to enter. She should have taken the stairs.

"Hold the door!" It was the incredibly attractive man who'd just moved in.

Verna willed the doors shut, but he was fast and slipped in as they were closing. "That was close. Thanks for trying. My name is Jeff. I believe I'm your next-door neighbor." He held out a leather-gloved hand.

She studied his mesmerizing eyes and wavy black hair. "Yes, well, I pushed the open-door button, but I guess it isn't working again." She reached out and gently held his hand. "Nice to meet you, Jeff. Welcome to the building, and you do live next door to me."

"And who is 'me'?" He released her hand and offered her an electric grin.

This was feeling like one of those sweet romantic movies. They would get stuck in the elevator, get to know each other, and realize they were soulmates. "Verna."

"Verna? That's a pretty name."

"I was named after my Italian grandmother." She tucked her hands deep into her pockets and willed the elevator to move faster. What if this man was a killer and this was the last elevator ride of her life? He oozed charm that she hoped wasn't an act.

The elevator felt full with Jeff next to her. "I'm named after my German grandfather. Is there a coffee shop nearby? I haven't gotten my pumpkin latte this season."

"The Rumble Cup is the best in town. I work there," Verna added. She blushed.

"Well, you would know. Are you going there right now?" He zipped his black snow jacket.

"Yes, I have an extra shift today. We're busy this time of year." She couldn't tear herself away from his electric jade eyes.

"I bet it's busy. Is it nearby?" He wrapped a green plaid holiday scarf around his neck and met her gaze.

She almost forgot to breathe when their eyes met. The worn green carpet compelled her attention. A strange sense of loss broke their connection, or was it a warning? Was he too good to be true? "Right down the street to your left. I'm on my way there now. It's close enough to walk."

"I hope you don't mind if I tag along. I was informed my new job is nearby, on the left. What a great coincidence."

The elevator rattled to a stop, and the doors creaked open. Fresh air seeped in and cooled Verna's hot cheeks as she hurried out. "No, I don't mind. Where do you work?"

He followed her, maintaining their proximity. "The fire department. I'm a paramedic. Coming from a busy city, I'm now eager to settle down and become more involved with the community."

Verna's shoulders relaxed. She'd made it out of the elevator alive. He must not be a serial killer preying on young women who rode elevators. "It's a great town, been here my whole life. My parents run the coffee shop. Mom and I added a small bakery to it. My specialty is cookies."

"My specialty is eating cookies." Jeff laughed and opened the glass door that opened onto the town's main street. The air was icy, and dark clouds threatened snow.

"My mom will like you." Oh, great, he'll think I want him to meet my family after an elevator ride. Besides, he had to already have a girl-friend or wife. "Mom likes everyone who has a healthy appetite."

"Sounds like my mom. This year, they're going on a holiday cruise to the Caribbean for their fortieth anniversary. Never been outside our state. Took some convincing and the gift of tickets to get them to go. This is the first year I'll be solo for the holidays, but getting settled will keep me busy."

He towered over her, and she could easily picture herself in his arms. "What a wonderful gift for them. My parents also rarely travel. Their thirty-fifth is next year. I hope they get to do something like that."

"Morning, Verna!" Mr. Hobble from the hardware store called out with a wave.

"Morning, Mr. Hobble!" Verna waved back.

He placed the sale sign on the sidewalk. "I'll be by for my coffee and holiday croissant. Make sure you save one for me."

"Will do."

Jeff slipped in next to her so they were walking side by side. "You're popular around here."

Verna quickened her step, and he smoothly matched it. "To those who eat or need their caffeine, I am."

Jeff cleared his throat. "Are you . . . well, are you taken?"

Verna almost tripped. "I—taken? No, I have little time to date, if that's what you're asking."

He shrugged and appeared more uncomfortable than Verna felt. It caught her attention, and she found it attractive. "That is what I'm attempting to ask."

"Single," Verna confirmed. "You?"

His grin returned. "Single. Would you like to show me around town and grab dinner later?"

Verna's heart skipped a beat. "I . . . well, I'm so busy, but I have the day after Christmas off."

He let out what sounded like a relieved sigh. "That's perfect. Today I'm going to the fire station and getting acquainted. I won't report for another week. Gives me time to explore."

"I can show you where everything is, and we have a great little diner that makes the best burgers and milkshakes, if you like that type of food. I do."

"My favorite."

"Of course, my parents could need me. Then I wouldn't be able to." What would he want with a plain, small-town girl like her? Besides, it was the holidays, and she was busy paying her bills.

"I'll ask them if it's okay." The wind caught his scarf, and he rewound it.

"What? No, that's not necessary. I do have the day off. I was just saying if one of them got sick or something and they needed me. We're almost here." Verna pointed to the lit-up sign with tinsel smothering it.

Jeff shook his head. "If there's an emergency, I'll take a rain check. You ice skate? It's something I did as a boy."

Verna hadn't skated in years. That wouldn't be a good look for her. "Yes, there's a place right outside of town, but I don't think—"

A red pickup screeched around the corner, and Verna and Jeff turned right as it veered off the road and came directly at them.

"Look out!" Jeff yelled and tried to shield her with his body in front of the building, but Verna slipped on the ice and slid toward the truck. Jeff reached for her, but the truck found her first. Pain shot up her right leg as she went airborne. She met Jeff's wide-eyed gaze for only a second as the truck found its way back to the road and disappeared. She landed hard with a sickening thump.

He was immediately at her side. "Verna! Talk to me. Where do you hurt?"

"I'm okay." She smiled, but her vision was dimming. He was already taking her pulse. She was in expert hands with a paramedic by her side. "My right leg hurts and—" She felt Jeff's coat cover her and blacked out.

————

She awoke and snuggled deeper in her flannel snowman sheets. "Thank goodness it was only a dream, Johnny. So crazy. I've never been hit or even almost hit by a truck, but the rest of the dream is how I met Jeff."

The alarm clock blared, and she shut it off in anticipation. Outside it was snowing hard, but that didn't put a damper on her day. It was finally here—Christmas Eve, the day she would become Jeff's wife.

She tugged on her favorite purple sweatpants and ugly sweater, which had a tree that lit up. A gift from Jeff the year before. She filled the cat's bowls and pulled on her snow boots. "Next time you see me, Johnny, I'll be a married woman. Jeff and his sweet kitty, Tessie, will be living with us since we have a three-bedroom and they only have one bedroom. You'd better behave and share your toys."

She bundled up to withstand the icy walk to her parents' house, where she'd dress for the ceremony and head to the church. Stepping outside her door, she ran into Jeff. He covered his eyes. "Isn't it bad luck to see the bride on the wedding day?"

"It is. But no one says you can't ride an elevator with me or take a stroll, right? That is, if you don't look at me." Verna grasped his gloved hand.

Jeff studied his snow boots with a grin. "Very true. Never heard any rules on that. How about kissing my fiancée? I promise to close my eyes."

Verna's stomach tingled like it did every time she was around him. "I have no problem with that, either."

They were interrupted by the clunk of the elevator stopping and the door slowly opening.

"Okay, I'm looking away. You lead us," Jeff said, focused on the ground.

Walking in the snowstorm felt like a romantic movie moment. "This is so perfect. It doesn't seem real." She squeezed Jeff's hand, but something tugged at her. What was she forgetting? All her stuff was at her parents'. Her bridesmaids would do her hair and makeup. What was it?

A truck barreled around the corner at high speed, like in her dream. Tires squealing, it went into a spin and was coming right for them. Verna gasped, and Jeff pushed her against the wall. But like in the dream, she slipped on a patch of ice from the dripping gutter and slid toward the out-of-control red truck. In a moment of clarity, she watched the truck hit her.

The last thing she heard was Jeff shouting her name before everything went black.

———

A baby's cry pierced her comfortable slumber. She reached for the spot where Johnny used to lie. She still missed that cat. She'd get a new cat . . . someday.

Jeff gently shook her arm. "Honey! Wake up. Timmy has a hundred-and-three fever."

Verna shot out of bed and bolted to their son's room. "He's burning up and pulling at his ear. We need to get him to the ER. This can't wait until morning."

Jeff grimaced. "The roads aren't plowed, but my truck will make it. Bundle him, and let's go."

Timmy cried through the elevator ride. The speakers were playing the stale Christmas music she used to find so fun. Tonight it grated on her nerves. The icy air took her breath away, and she wrapped the baby tighter in his blanket.

Jeff reached out his arms. "Hand me Timmy, and be careful crossing the street."

The snow was blowing sideways, making it almost a complete whiteout. Verna stepped off the buried curb into the street. Jeff had the truck door open and was climbing in with the baby to secure him in his car seat.

"I have his pacifier and—" Verna started as a truck sped around the corner.

The red truck went into a spin as she hurried to get out of its way, but she wasn't quick enough. It was a direct hit, sending her airborne toward their pickup. Its taillights were the last thing she saw. Jeff screamed her name, and Timmy had stopped crying. Her world went dark.

———

Verna rubbed the sleep from her eyes and reached for Jeff. The welcome aroma of coffee let her know where he was. What a dream. Everything had happened but that red pickup truck. She had hated it when Tim got those ear infections, but he'd outgrown them. Today was his wedding day. How was it possible that her baby was getting married? After she showered and put herself together so she could be a presentable mother of the groom, she found a platter of pancakes and bacon waiting for her next to her steaming coffee.

Jeff softly kissed her cheek. Her paramedic was as handsome as when they first met, when he moved into the building. Although he had white peppering his temples and a small potbelly, he'd barely aged. She had begun to show that age with wrinkles and fat that found places in her body to accentuate. The mirror only made her cringe now. Soon Jeff would retire, she'd sell the café, and they would finally buy a house and live in the country. Better late than never.

"Morning, sleepyhead. Happy anniversary." Two dozen red roses and a balloon graced the table.

"Happy anniversary! Thanks for getting breakfast done, and for the beautiful flowers and balloon. We'll celebrate in style after the wedding." Verna bent to smell the fragrant roses.

Jeff pulled her into a hug. "I celebrate each day I'm with you."

"You're a sweet talker. Sorry it took me so long. It takes a while at my age to look this good." Verna smoothed her newly cut hair. It had been hard to part with her long waves, but she loved her new layered hair, and so did Jeff.

"You are beautiful the moment you wake up. I already ate, so help yourself. Now it's time for the old man to spruce up too."

"Sissy's parents make me feel old. Glad they're hosting this and not us." Verna loaded her plate with bacon and two pumpkin pancakes.

"Well, they had her in their twenties. We were lucky to have Timmy, and if it took until you were forty, so be it. Tim was a blessing, and now we'll have a daughter. Next step: grandparents."

"Shh, not ready for that title yet." Verna took a bite of Jeff's fluffy pancakes. He made the best around.

Jeff wiggled his eyebrows. "You'll be the best-looking grandma ever."

"Hardly. Go take a shower, and clean your eyes out while you're at it."

Jeff laughed and hurried into their room. Verna inhaled her pancakes and washed down her bacon with holiday-flavored coffee. She loved that the kids were getting married on Christmas Eve like she and Jeff had, but something felt off. She felt it deep in her gut that they shouldn't leave their home today. But that was crazy. She couldn't miss seeing her son get married.

Jeff stepped out in his black tux.

Verna caught her breath. "You look like you should be the groom."

"I agree." Jeff pulled out a small red box and handed it to her.

"I thought we agreed no gifts this year." Verna held the box, which promised jewelry.

"No, I agreed you wouldn't buy *me* a gift. Open it." His expression was filled with expectation.

"I should have known you'd find a way around it." Inside the black box, perched on white velvet, was the most perfect white pearl ring she'd ever seen. On each side were two small diamonds. "It's beautiful. Although I don't need jewelry."

Jeff shook his head. "Need has nothing to do with it. I'm showing you how thankful I am that we found each other that night when I first moved here, that your family welcomed me. And when you said yes to being my wife—well, I've been blessed. Plus, your patience through all those years trying to become a parent and dealing with my crazy hours. A guy needs to show he's grateful for all he has occasionally. Today is our day and our son's. What could be more perfect? The ring represents that, and it's the gem for this year. I checked."

A single tear escaped Verna's eye. She quickly wiped it away. "Don't get me crying already. We haven't taken pictures. I agree, we're blessed. Now I'm going to slip into my dress and fix my makeup."

Soon they were in the elevator, their favorite holiday song playing.

"May I have this dance?" Jeff bowed and held out his hand.

"Of course." Verna giggled like she was a young girl again.

They danced through four floors and well past when the door opened. As they stepped out, their neighbor Sam clapped.

"Off to the wedding? Give Timmy and Sissy my best wishes. Wish I could be there, but I have a plane to catch to see the kids. Merry Christmas," Sam said, closing his mailbox.

"He understands. Merry Christmas, Sam." Verna hugged him before they stepped outside.

Jeff squeezed her hand. "You want to wait here while I get the car? I had to park it down the street."

A light snow fell, and Verna clutched her silver dress to keep it clean while trekking through the snow in her old boots. She would put on her dress shoes at the church. "No, nothing as romantic as walking in the snow."

When they got to the end of the block, they cautiously looked both ways and began to cross the street. A familiar truck raced around the corner.

"Look out!" Jeff yelled.

As he tugged them back to the curb, the red truck slid sideways, and Verna slipped in a patch of ice. Jeff reached for her but missed. The truck hit her with a loud thump.

"Verna!" Jeff's voice was the last thing she heard.

————

Verna rolled over, expecting to cuddle with Jeff, but he wasn't there. That dream had been a painful reminder of happier days, when her son got married. And it ended with that truck hitting her again.

Although it was her anniversary, it wasn't a happy day. Today she'd finally spread Jeff's ashes. Tomorrow she'd celebrate Christmas with Timmy, Sissy, and the girls. At seven and eight years old, Natalie and Piper still believed in Santa's magic. Verna wished Santa had some magic for her. Her wish was to be with Jeff.

After he died from an unexpected heart attack at the end of last summer, she sold their dream house and moved back to the building where they met. She lived in the one-bedroom apartment Jeff had moved into. It was a lonely full circle. And something was haunting her, tugging at the edge of her moments. Like she knew what was coming, but how could she?

She sighed and pulled on black sweatpants with silver glitter. The matching top had Santa drinking coffee in Paris. Jeff had bought it for her on their last Christmas together, with the promise that they would do that next year. She pulled on her gray coat and gloves, picked up the box that had contained her husband for the last several months, and stepped onto the elevator. Remembering how they used to dance to the music, she held him close, but the updated elevator was silent, mirroring her life. She would scatter him at the park where they used to walk together, by the gazebo where the wildflowers bloomed.

"I'll come with you, Mom," Timmy had said over a morning call. "I have a rare day off."

"You enjoy that day off, son. I can do this. I insist. Spend some time with your family."

His voice sounded relieved when he accepted. Verna would take the short walk to the park and back. Later, she'd call and get a ride to spend Christmas with her loved ones. She didn't drive anymore, which was one of the reasons she'd moved back to town.

If only she hadn't hung on to the café for all these years because it reminded her of her parents. It couldn't compete with the chain that moved in. It had drained them financially, and they never got to Paris, but at least they had their dream home for a few years. Now all her dreams were gone, other than her son, his wife, and two grandchildren. She felt guilty that she'd rather be with her husband than her family.

A red truck flashed through her mind. Why was it a constant presence in her dreams? Did it represent something? Maybe change or a new start? Or did it mean to be careful with what she did? She shook her head and stepped off the elevator, expecting to see Jeff or even her old neighbor Sam in the lobby. Neither was there. She was the only one left. A sadness crept through her soul, although she was grateful for all the good memories.

She pushed into the chilled December air, hugging her husband's remains. She straightened her shoulders and moved forward with a heaviness in her stomach. As she crossed the street, snow fell, triggering a warning. A red truck sped around the corner like in her dreams. She clung to Jeff serenely as it hit her. A sense of peace filled her as she flew into the air and all went dark.

———————

Verna woke up and threw on the old ratty bathrobe she'd borrowed from her mother. She'd had that dream about getting hit by a red truck again. It always involved a handsome man named Jeff. But none of that mattered. She shuffled into the kitchen to feed Johnny. She had one more shift at her parent's coffee shop and Christmas morning with her parents. There was no man in her life, and she wondered if there ever would be after her last awful experience with a cheater. A small-town girl who does what? Nothing? Yup, that was the old her. This was the new Verna. The snow fell harder as she slipped into her festive shirt and jeans.

She petted Johnny. "Who's going to go out in this mess? I'll call and see if they even need me."

The call gave her a day off.

"You bring Johnny over later and spend the night. I'm making my famous cioppino, and we'll go to church later," Mom said.

A weight had been lifted from her. She browsed the colorful travel brochures she had been collecting. Paris was where she wanted to go. She had lived frugally and stuck to her budget, even at Christmas. She reviewed her savings, which would be useful. At last she made the call and was scheduled to go on December 26. Now to tell her parents.

Everything felt so different at that moment, like she was finally doing what she was supposed to. That life she dreamed of had never existed, and her dream death had to mean she needed to change, start over. Right? The man from her dreams was everything she desired, but he was just a dream.

Instead of going out, she baked snickerdoodles. There was a loud boom, and outside her window, she saw a terrible accident. A red truck was speeding off, and someone was lying on the ground. People gathered around. A chill shot through her. A *red* pickup truck. The same red pickup that always hit her in her dreams. Maybe staying home had saved her life, but who took her place? No, it was a silly dream and a mere coincidence that someone got hit by a red truck.

"I hope they're okay," Verna said. Johnny closed his eyes, unaffected. The timer went off, and she tried to put the accident out of her mind. She retrieved cookies that not only smelled good but were visually appealing enough to sell at her parents' shop. "Perfect."

She made a platter to take to Sam and his new wife, Dottie. They were always so kind to her and would watch and feed Johnny if she needed them to. After that delivery, a man called from the doorway next to hers. "Good morning! I'm Jeff, new to the area and looking for a good cup of coffee. Any suggestions?"

Verna almost passed out. The guy from her dreams. Couldn't be. "I, um . . . "

He rushed toward her. "Are you okay?"

"Yes. All this baking, and I forgot to eat. My family runs a coffee shop, but I have coffee and cookies at my place if you're interested. And my name is Verna." She blushed. Was picking up a strange man wise? Even if he was from her dreams. Well, Sam was across the way if she got into trouble.

"If it's not too much trouble, Verna. I got my furniture moved in and haven't gone shopping yet. I can't function without my coffee."

"Well, it's the least I can do for a new neighbor."

"I owe you one. I was supposed to start as a paramedic at the firehouse, but the snow caused a delay until next year. They told me to enjoy some time off because I'll be busy from then on. I was on the phone doing something crazy." Jeff followed her into the apartment, where Johnny rubbed against him.

"What was that?" Verna shut the door and hurried into the kitchen.

"I booked a flight to Paris. Always wanted to go there, and now I can see the holiday decorations. Crazy, isn't it? Sure wiped out my savings, but why not?"

Verna's jaw dropped. "You're kidding me! I did the same thing." Curiosity got the better of her, and she cautiously peeked out the window to see what was happening. The ambulance crew was loading an older woman.

"What? How weird is that?" Jeff grinned.

"Meant to be?" Verna couldn't pull her eyes away from the accident victim being loaded into the ambulance.

"Yes," he whispered.

The paramedic stepped aside, and the woman's face was exposed. Verna turned back to Jeff, but he was gone. This couldn't be!

The memories rushed back. The red pickup. The dreams. The urn. She had been reliving her life. The old lady hit by the truck was *her*.

An angel stepped into the room. She had long black hair and startlingly alert brown eyes. "Welcome, Verna. Do you remember what happened?"

"I know I reexperienced my life in my dreams, with a red truck mixed in. Then a real red truck hit me when I went to scatter Jeff's ashes, and I watched the accident from here in a life that didn't happen. Am I dead?"

The angel's gown flowed around her like a caressing ocean wave. Her voice was a gentle, soothing ripple. "Yes, you are, Verna. You were in a coma, where you got to enjoy the good times in your life, but the one bad one that landed you in the hospital was mixed in. That last life was not yours, but it helped you watch the real accident from a distance. These dreams prepared you to come home—after a small trip."

"A trip?" Verna watched her familiar surroundings disappear.

"A trip to Paris is overdue. Afterward, numerous individuals are excited to see you once more, including your parents, but not everyone could wait." The angel grinned and laid a soothing hand on Verna's shoulder, and then she was in an empty hospital room.

Jeff stepped out of the white light that pulsed behind the angel. He was about the age he'd been when they met. Verna gasped, unable to speak. Holding her close, he pressed his lips against hers in a tender kiss. He pulled away and asked the angel, "It's okay if I kiss my wife, isn't it?"

"Of course it is."

Verna's eyes widened. "Oh, Jeff! I'm so happy to see you, but what about our son and grandkids? I've ruined their Christmas by dying like this."

"No, they were with you when you died. They made their peace and will be okay, I promise. Tim knows you're with Jeff now." The angel radiated harmony.

Verna leaned into Jeff, absorbing that familiar love. "What about the person that hit me?"

The angel shook her head. "He is not a good person. He left and will live with his actions. His excessive drinking and mistreatment of his wife are terrible. He must face the consequences. Do not worry about him."

A church bell rang twelve times. "It's Christmas, right?" Verna grasped Jeff's hand.

"It is," the angel replied.

"Merry Christmas, sweetheart, and happy belated anniversary," Jeff said.

The world she knew disappeared, and they were standing in Paris, ready to begin a new adventure.

AUTHOR'S NOTE

THANK you for sharing this Christmas journey with me! I wrote these stories during the holiday season in 2023 so I could soak in the season's magic. I was pleased that Zelina the angel made an appearance in the final story. As my family is aware, I *love* Christmas. I watch Christmas movies year-round, decorate the house before Thanksgiving, and never miss an annual re-reading of "A Christmas Carol." As much as I enjoy the sweet holiday stories on a popular channel, I was unable to write those lighthearted stories. This collection has my twist where bad happens yet good comes out of it. Plus, there's a surprise for the people closest to me over the years, along with the ones whose help was invaluable in completing this collection. Their names are *randomly* given to characters whether they are human, animal, or supernatural.

I also included a Christmas bonus short story *The Bike* from "In the Tree's Shadow" along with an excerpt from "A Long Walk Home" following About the Author.

May you find your miracle or a friendly ghost not only during the holiday season but year-round. Embrace that inner child and let your unique light sparkle. Merry Christmas and Happy Holidays!

ABOUT THE AUTHOR

D. L. Finn is an independent California local who encourages everyone to embrace their inner child. She was born and raised in the foggy Bay Area, but in 1990 she relocated with her husband, kids, dogs, and cats to Nevada City, in the Sierra foothills. She immersed herself in reading all types of books but especially loved romance, horror, and fantasy. She always treasured creating her own reality on paper. Finally, surrounded by towering pines, oaks, and cedars, her creativity was nurtured until it bloomed. Her creations include children's books, adult fiction, and poetry. She continues on her adventure with an open invitation to all readers to join her.

THE BIKE

BONUS SHORT STORY FROM: IN THE TREE'S SHADOW

TWELVE-YEAR-OLD BILLY STARTED his day filled with the Christmas spirit. He took the Number 3 bus to downtown Laceyville. Barely a dot on the map, but it was where you went if you needed something. Mom was working her last shift at the small diner down the road. Little Joey stayed with old Mrs. Trumbold, who had a never-ending supply of sugar cookies and milk. On special occasions, she'd add some chocolate chips to the cookies.

Billy sat in the middle of the bus. There were only two other people sitting in the back. Everyone minded their business, so he enjoyed the holiday decorations through the scratched-up window. Every house had a tree in the front window covered in silver tinsel and colored lights. The bus jolted to a stop right in front of Harvey's Department Store. Billy clutched his dingy sock full of change and dollar bills and followed a sour older man who smelled of horse manure and cheese to the bus's side door. The man eyed him like Billy might knock him down.

The store was glowing. Covered in red and green holiday decorations, it was full of last-minute shoppers. His mom had brought him and his little brother here to take in the holiday cheer and visit Santa a few weeks ago. He knew Santa was hired help in a red suit, but Joey still believed in all that magic. Billy wisely asked for new clothes, knowing he'd be lucky to get that, but Joey requested a new red bike.

His mom's eyes filled with tears after looking at the bike's price tag. He knew twenty-five dollars was more than she could afford. She didn't make that much working at the diner, where tips were meager. At least they'd get some chocolate candies in their stocking and a warm secondhand coat.

Billy had been earning extra cash mowing lawns and cleaning garages over the last several months. His mom wanted to take him to the bank and start a savings account, but he was halfway to getting the Sting-Ray bike all his friends had. Of course, none of that mattered now because Billy became the man of the house after his father died from cancer eleven months ago. He would use his money to get his little brother what he'd asked Santa for and have enough left to get Mom something nice, like his dad used to do. He could always earn enough to get what he wanted by next summer.

Billy dodged a large woman whose arms were filled with toy trucks and dolls. Lucky kids. He headed to where the bikes were, but the red one was gone. In its place was a blue model that was ten dollars more —eight more dollars than he had.

"Look out, kid." The lady pushed past him. "I'll take that bike too," she told the smiling saleswoman, who was dressed as Mrs. Claus.

"You are fortunate! That's our last bike."

Billy stood in line and inquired about the display bike in the window.

Mrs. Claus patted his head. "That has a dent on it, son. We need to fix it in Santa's workshop before it can be sold."

Billy shook his head. "A dent is okay. I have twenty-five dollars for it."

The woman reached around him and grabbed a scarf from a lady holding a screaming baby. "Sorry, that's against store policy. It would make the store look bad to sell damaged inventory. Buy something else. I have customers to wait on."

Billy sighed loudly. Joey would be so disappointed. Still, he was determined to add a few gifts under the decorated fig tree. A turquoise scarf and gloves set with a peacock feather design would be perfect for his mom, along with pink slippers, a robe, and a cheesy romance novel. He found a fire truck, a football, a new adventure book, new Christmas PJs, and slippers for his brother. The family always used to wear matching PJs on Christmas Eve, way back when life was normal and cancer hadn't taken away all its joy.

He added a package of SweeTarts to his purchases. That left him with enough change to ride the bus home. But when he stepped on the Number 3, he found the change gone and a hole in his pocket.

"No money, no ride." The red-haired driver had not been gifted with the Christmas spirit.

Billy bowed his head and retreated in embarrassment from the bus where no goodwill existed.

He ran to the store to look for his lost change, but the door was locked. A young man with braces and a red Santa hat took the dented bike out of the window display, ignoring Billy's pounding on the door.

"Guess I'm walking home."

Billy took the shortcut that passed the back of the store. The employee who had ignored him brought the bike out the back door. He tugged on the door that said Do Not Enter.

"Great, it's locked!" He dropped the bike and stomped back into the store.

The dim lights illuminated the red bike like it was on display. It would be perfect for his little brother. Billy pushed his bags full of gifts on his shoulders and did something he'd never done before. He stole the bike.

He had almost escaped the dark lot when a male voice screamed. "Stop, thief!"

Billy's stomach was heavy, but all it took was the thought of his brother's face on Christmas morning. His long legs kept pedaling on the small bike. Although he was a criminal now, he tried a deal he thought God might accept. "Please forgive me. If you let me keep it for Joey, I promise to pay the store back more than they were charging."

Turning onto the main road, he wove in and out of traffic. The icy wind pounded his face, and his thin coat offered no protection from the approaching winter storm. He tried to convince himself that what he had done was okay until guilt crashed down on him.

"Sorry, Joey. This isn't right."

Billy turned the bike around in the intersection as a bus barreled around the corner with its horn blaring. Everything in front of him went black except for a beautiful angel with long, ebony hair and sea-green wings.

That was the last thing he remembered until he smelled cheese, garlic, and bread. He carefully opened his eyes, expecting the angel again, but a kind-faced man was at his side.

Billy blurted out his story while the man gently shook his head and rubbed his chin but withheld comment.

"I've got to get the bike back to them, sir. It doesn't belong to me."

The man smiled. "That bike is dinged up, but it's yours."

Billy wondered if he was dreaming. "It's what?"

"My friend Officer Doyle told me you took it. I figured you had your reasons, so I offered to pay. The store manager gladly accepted. Although you aren't allowed in the store anymore unless an adult accompanies you." His smile was as gentle as his eyes.

Billy's eyes widened. "Why would you do that, mister?"

The man, who had to be as old as his mom, patted his arm softly. "Everyone deserves a second chance, and a young man like yourself should be with his family on Christmas Eve, not in jail. And please call me Mr. Jones."

"My name is Billy, Mr. Jones. But I spent all my money on these probably ruined presents." Billy pointed to the two bags on the table next to the red bench he was lying on.

When he grinned, Mr. Jones had creases around his eyes like his dad. "Your gifts are fine—not even a scratch on the fire truck."

Billy held back tears. "How can I pay you back?"

"I could use help around here on Saturdays and maybe sometimes after school. You could work off your bike. If everything goes well, I'll hire you permanently."

"Really? Gee, that would be great!" Billy sat up and winced as his head throbbed more. He was sore, but everything worked.

Mr. Jones pointed to his head. "That bump on your head will hurt you for a while, but the doctor said you'd be fine."

Billy looked around. "A doctor was here?"

"Yes, picking up a pizza to take home. Very lucky he was here so you didn't have to go to the hospital."

"Yes, lucky. Thank you."

"You're welcome. Now get up slowly, Billy, and gather your things. I'll take you and that bike home."

Billy jumped down to a sticky red tile floor. "You don't have to do more, Mr. Jones. I can ride the bike home, and you can be with your family."

A sad look crossed the man's face. "I lost my wife last year in a car accident. We were never blessed with kids, so you would be doing me a favor if you allowed me the holiday cheer of being able to return you to your family."

"Sorry, Mr. Jones. My dad died too." Billy inspected the man. He wasn't horrible looking, and a widower too. Maybe . . .

When they pulled in front of his house, his mother was talking to a police officer.

Billy stepped out of the truck with a loud gulp. "You should meet my mom, Mr. Jones. I know she'd like to thank you for all your help."

"I—"

"Billy!" She engulfed him in a tight hug. "Are you okay? What were you thinking? You are grounded for two weeks—" She stopped when she saw Mr. Jones. "Officer Doyle told me what you did for him, Mr. . . . "

"Jones, but call me Mike. It was my pleasure to help." His new friend's brown eyes twinkled, and Mom's cheeks took on an odd shade of pink.

"My name is Maria. Nice to meet you, Mike." She held out her hand, which Mr. Jones engulfed in his large ones. The handshake went on longer than most.

"Nice to meet you, Maria. You raised him well. He was going to make things right after doing something so stupid. With your permission, he's agreed to help at my restaurant to pay off his debt. The road wasn't so kind, but the bus missed him. He's a fortunate young man."

"We were extremely lucky tonight, thank you. And of course you have my permission. I made a fresh pot of coffee. Would you like a cup?" Mom smoothed her wavy, dark brown hair and smiled.

Mr. Jones finally let go of his mom's hand as Officer Doyle walked by and waved. "Don't do that again, young man. You won't get so lucky next time. Happy holidays."

"I won't, sir. Merry Christmas!" Billy said.

Officer Doyle shook his head and winked at Mr. Jones before getting into his car.

"Good advice, Billy. I don't want to impose on your family celebration, Maria. Maybe another—"

Billy interrupted him before he could decline, much to his mom's obvious embarrassment.

"Mr. Jones is alone. Can't we invite him to our Christmas Eve dinner tonight?"

Her face relaxed. "It would be an honor if you joined us. Our way of paying back your kindness."

Mr. Jones nodded as Joey raced out of Mrs. Trumbold's house and threw himself into Billy's aching arms. Mr. Jones retrieved the bike, wrapped in a blanket, and followed Billy's mom into the garage.

The dent and the scratches went unnoticed Christmas morning, and it turned out to be a good Christmas, even though Billy missed his dad. Mr. Jones stayed for that dinner too and many more to follow.

Money worries became a thing of the past when Maria took over the paperwork in Mr. Jones's busy restaurant. It took over a year, but Mr. Jones became a part of the family. Maria cut back from working full-time to part-time after she announced they were expecting a baby, due on Christmas Day.

The baby arrived on the night when miracles happen—Christmas Eve. Not that anyone would believe it, but Billy saw the same beautiful angel standing next to his baby sister's crib, the one from the night the bus narrowly missed him. She smiled and waved at him, then disappeared.

EXCERPT FROM: A LONG WALK HOME

THE SUN HAD JUST SET under dark gray clouds. The night chill was creeping through Kenzie's new red coat, making her shiver. Sidewalks were overflowing with people trying to avoid the forecasted snow. "The storm of the century" had been the main topic at work. The local news and her newspaper's "weather specialist," Rod, were predicting a blizzard that would shut the city down. *Be prepared.* She wasn't worried, but her boss, Eileen, had let everyone go early to beat the snow, closing the office halfway through what was already a half day—Christmas Eve—even though the storm wasn't supposed to hit until that evening. Eileen probably just wanted to get out of there, like everyone else. Except Kenzie.

"Ho, ho, ho! A storm is coming, everyone. Go finish up your shopping," Eileen announced, without looking in Kenzie's direction. She added, "Then get home and enjoy your time with your loved ones. Happy holidays!"

I'll get right on that, Eileen. There was no shopping for her to do because there were no loved ones to spend Christmas with.

Kenzie hung around the empty office editing some feel-good articles about animals and children for the coming year. She could be so positive and upbeat in her writing, but not in her own life, apparently.

At least her column was set through February, but that brought her no satisfaction. Finally, she ran out of things to do. It was time to go home and endure her four-day weekend.

Kenzie rubbed her cold hands together, wishing she hadn't left her new white gloves—a gift from Eileen—on her desk. She sighed and pushed her way through the last-minute holiday shoppers. An older woman toting two large bags ran right into her.

"Hey!" Kenzie exclaimed, stumbling.

The woman hurried away without a single glance back.

"Don't mind me!" Kenzie yelled.

No response, not even from the people rushing past her. *Whatever! Hurry home to your happy lives.* Jaws clenched, Kenzie shoved her way through the holiday nightmare. A few months ago, being unseen would have been a welcome state. How nice it would have been to avoid all those looks of pity right after her breakup with Heath. She'd avoided the good-intentioned questions because she had no answers. Why *would* Heath leave her for the person who claimed to be her best friend? Kenzie frowned. *How could life get any worse?* No, she didn't dare ask that question.

Even with the rudeness she encountered, she was content to be walking home instead of taking the bus. Her car would be in the shop until after the New Year getting a rebuilt transmission. Maybe five long blocks in the crisp, cold air would dispel her Grinchy mood. Doubtful, but worth a try.

————

Kenzie was so deep in her thoughts she didn't notice the man with long brown hair and bright green eyes bundled in a long, black wool coat directly behind her. He matched her every step, including her run-in with the holiday shopper. The woman may have ignored Kenzie, but she noticed him and gave a forced smile. He knew the woman was worried about her son. She was rushing to the hospital with his gifts, unsure if he would make it through the night. Unfortunately, it would be the last Christmas they would spend together. The son would recover from his car accident, but she would have a stroke right after

Valentine's Day and wouldn't pull through. He sighed and kept following Kenzie.

———

Once Kenzie navigated her way past the crowded stores, there were the cheerfully decorated restaurants and bars. She knew that among all that holiday cheer was Heath's favorite sports bar, Sporty's Spread, where she used to meet him after work. Sometimes he showed up, and sometimes he didn't. She'd learned to bring work or a book to read on those dates. Kenzie wondered if Heath and her former best friend, Joy, would be there celebrating their upcoming nuptials.

In just a few weeks, Heath and Joy went from dating to engaged. Okay, maybe Kenzie and Heath had done the same thing, but the one thing Kenzie couldn't get past was the day they'd chosen to get married. *This* Christmas—the same day Kenzie and Heath had planned on tying the knot. *Who picks the same day to get married—but to a different girl?* Heath did. She knew it hadn't been Joy's idea; she was a person who never decorated for Christmas and hardly bought gifts. The original idea for a Christmas wedding had been Kenzie's. It used to be her favorite day of the year.

Looking back, though, there had been many warning signs. She'd always thought it was odd that she hadn't met Heath's family. *You will at the wedding,* was always his response. She'd kept brushing away the feeling at the pit of her stomach, that warning, when she dealt with Heath. He made it seem so normal when he didn't return her calls.

"I'm just so busy, babe. But someday, I'll be able to treat you like a princess."

Miss a date, same excuse, but he'd show up later at her apartment, waking her up. She always welcomed him with a tired smile, which he never noticed. His self-absorption and lack of involvement even extended to their wedding. He allowed her to make all the plans, including putting the deposits on her credit card. He was far too busy to call back or take care of them in person.

"Thanks, babe. Soon we'll have the same bank accounts, and money won't matter. You know how busy I am at work. I'm the boss's right-hand man. Gonna make so much money from this sale, and then it'll be all first class after that."

So she racked up bills and planned the wedding while he worked. The only good thing about that was that she was able to get all her deposits refunded except one. That $150 ate away at her. She even considered suing him, but she didn't want to see him again. Too bad she'd been cocooned in her giddy stupidity of what she thought would be "happily ever after." Now she could see he hadn't been that into her, even when he proposed after they'd only been dating for a month. It was at Sporty's Spread, right after his favorite team, the New England Patriots, won the Super Bowl. She'd been secretly rooting for the Atlanta Falcons.

"Hey, babe. We have good jobs, get along, and love each other. What do you say we tie the knot?"

She couldn't believe she'd thought that had been romantic. She had only seen and heard what she wanted to. Although she did notice the extra attention he paid Joy—and every other good-looking woman. She convinced herself that he just liked to look. Five months later, she'd found out how wrong she'd been about that. Flirting was the one thing he managed to follow through on.

The sharp ringtone and vibration of her phone startled her from her thoughts. She quickly glanced at it and sighed, recognizing a familiar number. It was Sue calling again. She'd been trying to convince Kenzie to spend the holidays with her family for the last two weeks. Kenzie kept saying she wouldn't know until Christmas if she'd get the day off. *Working on a big article,* she lied to Sue over and over. *So much research to do. My big break.* She knew Sue didn't believe her and wouldn't give up, so she started ignoring the calls. She'd been ignoring a lot of calls over the past few months. Almost everyone had given up on her except Sue, who was still friends with both Kenzie and Joy.

Kenzie wanted to be alone. To mourn the death of her wedding and a chance at finally having love and a real family. Heath had filled her head with tales of perfect childhood holidays with his family, which was why, she thought, he had so quickly agreed to her choice of getting married on Christmas Day. She'd been clueless for the entire relationship, right up to the day she found out that he liked her "a lot" but wasn't in love with her.

So, of course, the next logical thing for him to do was start dating Joy. Yeah, Joy had asked if it was okay, and Kenzie had said yes, but she hadn't meant it. How could Joy not know that?

Kenzie rolled her eyes as she passed a beautiful, smiling couple walking together. She wondered when that man would wipe that smile off the woman's face. Then she'd have to live with the beautiful illusion of what had never been. *Another victim of sappy romance movies,* Kenzie thought. Was that giggling woman as desperate to be needed as Kenzie had been? She hoped not. Kenzie certainly wasn't going to fall for another movie-star handsome face and chiseled body that only produced excuses, fake promises, and hurt feelings.

Over the last few months, she'd gone through at least a case of tissues. Kenzie couldn't imagine she had any more tears left to shed. She'd stopped yelling at the off-white lace photo album, *Heath & Kenzie's Journey of Love*. The album and the tissues were now at the landfill—along with her happiness. She didn't accept any invitations, and she definitely didn't want to be set up with anyone. She wanted nothing more to do with romance, dating, and especially Christmas.

The Kenzie of years past had always been the one decorating the office, full of good cheer. She had believed in love. This year, in addition to avoiding all socializing, she excused herself from planning the office Christmas party—and from the event itself. No secret Santa, no shopping with friends, no charity work, no holiday baking—nothing. The queen of Christmas had gone into exile.

But staying busy until the holidays were over wasn't going to be easy. She'd been informed that her workplace was off limits to everyone over the weekend. Eileen had made sure to look at Kenzie when she made that announcement. So all that was left was binge-watching old holiday movies and ignoring the world. She'd start the New Year out right, though, just as soon as she got through the worst Christmas ever.

A tremor shot through Kenzie as she rushed past Sporty's Spread. She couldn't catch her breath as the familiar smell of barbecue reached her. The colorful buildings were squeezing the life out of her with their greasy cheer. She needed to get home and stay there until the holiday passed. She didn't need any reminders of Heath or the places he frequented. Kenzie darted out into the street to escape the memories.

Halfway across the street, she saw a light flash out of the corner of her eye. A blue car was seconds from hitting her. She barely jumped out of its way as it sped past her. The red taillights disappeared around the corner before she could get a license plate or make.

"Idiot!" she bellowed as her heart threatened to beat its way out of her chest.

She glanced around, hoping someone would inquire if she was all right. No one noticed that she'd almost been killed. She carefully made her way to the sidewalk and glanced back to where she'd almost been run over. Should she report it to the police? All she knew was the color of the car. It was the same color as Heath's BMW. It could have been another BMW or something similar. No, they wouldn't be interested in her complaint, she concluded.

The only thing she was sure of was that Heath wasn't driving. He was such a careful driver, to the point of always going under the speed limit, like someone with a learner's permit. *Never even had a ticket*, he always bragged. It had driven her nuts, so she always made sure she was the one driving. And yes, always the one paying for gas and parking too. She swallowed hard. Had he done that on purpose so she'd want to drive? What if she was wrong? Someone ran into her, stepping on her foot.

"Watch out!" she exclaimed.

An elderly man in a tan overcoat, carrying several packages, smiled brightly at her. "Sorry, miss. I didn't mean to bump into you. My fault."

Kenzie's eyes narrowed, but she didn't reply. He had scuffed her new red leather boot. Now she'd have to polish that out.

His smile didn't leave his round, bearded face. "Merry Christmas, miss." He nodded and hurried off without looking back.

"Whatever," she mumbled, moving down the sidewalk as fast as she could without running.

She'd only gone half a block when she felt her face redden. She bit her lower lip. It hadn't been necessary to treat that sweet old man like that, especially after he apologized. It wasn't his fault her ex was an idiot, her parents were dead, and she'd almost been run over. Kenzie massaged her temples. She needed to get home so she wouldn't say or do anything else she'd regret. She'd open that chardonnay she'd gotten on sale last week, fill her glass to the brim, and keep drinking until she forgot. *That's a good plan,* she thought.

———

The man with the green eyes smiled at the gentleman who had bumped into Kenzie. He was taking all those packages, filled with toys, to the homeless shelter to give some children and their families a bit of hope. Kenzie needed some of that hope too. He searched until he found the person he was looking for on the other side of the street. He caught the woman's attention with a flash of light, just as he had done to prevent Kenzie from being run over. The woman's mouth fell open. It worked. She had seen Kenzie.

He nodded to the red-headed female behind the shocked brunette. *What was her name? Oh yes, Olive.* It was too bad only he could see her. She was radiating pure beauty. He watched Olive whisper into the woman's ear, hopeful that her words would make a difference. He had not actually met Olive, but he had heard good things about her work. It made him believe the woman might respond positively to Olive's suggestions, even if she could not hear what was being said. He knew humans could feel their words, which filled him with great optimism.